THE DRAGON'S WRATH BOUNTY

PATRICK DUGAN

To my found family who love and support me.

H ere's to surviving the toughest bounty yet," Ayre said. The thief held his mug of ale up to the rest of the Shadow Blades in salute.

They all tapped their mugs and took a drink. "Here's to the next bounty," Jileli said. The blood mage set her mug down and looked at Saria. "There is a next bounty, right?"

With the two hundred gold they would soon receive for finding the Ashen Orb, Saria figured they could lay low for a year and enjoy life instead of chasing down monsters of all types. But after two weeks, she'd be bored, Ayre and Perric would be broke from the whorehouses, and who knew where Jileli and Lithia would be? She didn't yet know them well enough to guess how fast they'd spend that much money. "There is and now would be a good time to pick it."

Perric signaled the server to deliver another round. The paladin was in a good mood and another few ales would have him hugging everyone. "What's the rush? We should enjoy our good fortune." The Orb had been delivered and soon they would have the gold. With an amount this large, the

Mistress of Bounties wouldn't cover the amount from the organization coffers. The bounty requestor provided it when they came to collect the prize.

Saria glanced around the empty inn to see if anyone had wandered in. Between troop faires, the Dragon's Nest was quiet, but the establishment more than made up for it during the week the faire was in town.

So Perric wasn't wrong. What was the rush? They had over a week before the troops started filtering in. If they were spending freely when the other troops hadn't found the dagger, there could be suspicions. After all, the Blades hadn't gone to Tolle with the rest of the troops trying to win the bounty. Worse, if Gnedain showed up and lied about who'd attacked who in the forest last month, they would be in a compromised position. The itch between Saria's shoulder blades increased with each passing thought.

"Saria?" Lithia asked. The shadow fae archer looked concerned.

Saria shook her head to clear it. "Sorry, was considering Perric's question."

"And?" the archer asked.

"We should get out of Moonbourne. Too many questions if we are hanging around here. We collect our coin from the Mistress of Bounties, tell her what happened, and head for the hills. No sense sitting around for other troops to start looking for answers," Saria decided. She would also need to tell the Mistress what she'd discovered of her missing son, a private request Regina had made of Saria since they had known each other for decades.

"Good enough for me," Ayre said finishing off his ale.

They all sat quietly for a moment as the server delivered another round.

"In fact, let's go check the board." Saria rose and headed

toward the bounty board, which the established troops called it the baby board. Every inn across Southern Holm had their version, all locals looking for help. If you needed a harder job done, you paid to showcase your bounty at a faire.

Younger troops could survive on local jobs since they were close by and normally fairly easy. The main thing Saria was looking for was one that would get the Blades out of Moonbourne.

The board was picked over since it was between troop faires. Saria read each of the parchments pinned to the wall, bounties that had come in since they'd last checked.

Ayre pulled a bounty from the board and handed it to Saria. "We should take this one in Cloni. The night market is legendary."

While it would get them away from Moonbourne, it was not a good fit for their team given the distances involved. "I don't care what you've heard about the markets in Cloni. We aren't traipsing across the continent to take a bounty that won't even cover our expenses," Saria said.

"We could wait another week for the next faire," Perric suggested. He had second fresh pint of ale in his hand, even though it was before lunch.

"No," Saria said with a shake of her head. "We all know why we shouldn't be in Moonbourne that long. We collect our gold, pick a bounty, and get out of here in case there is any backlash."

Since last month's faire, the Blades had found out they'd been marked for assassination, killed most of the Skull Posse, and—through a secret spot of favoritism from the Mistress of Bounties they could never reveal—retrieved the Ashen Orb while all the other troops had been on a wild goose chase for a jeweled dagger. Any of those were enough to place the Blades into situations Saria didn't want to deal with. The two hundred gold would keep them solvent for a long while, but it was not enough to retire.

Jileli snatched a parchment down and handed it to Saria. "Missing person bounty. They were last seen in a town near Auano. We can stay out of sight while we chase it down."

Saria fingers tingled as she took the bounty. Not a lot to go on and not even worth a gold, which was why it was still there, but it kept the Blades away from trouble. After splitting two hundred gold, they could afford a less than profitable mission. Plus, Auano wasn't across the continent like Cloni. This was the right choice. "I agree."

"Really?" Lithia asked. "We could just return to Whitecrest and lay low for a while."

Saria checked around the group, lingering on Ayre and Perric. "Keeping people out of trouble would be far more challenging than taking a bounty."

"Understood," Lithia said with a grin.

"I'll go pay the vig and we can set off as soon as we are square on the first bounty."

Saria left the group to their own devices while she went to the bounty office. The hallway to the Mistress's office was empty this early in the day. Regina was writing in a large book when Saria stuck her head in. "I need to pay a vig."

"Saria, I was just about to come find you," she said with a wide grin. She closed the journal and slid it to the side. "Come in and close the door, please."

She did as requested and took a seat in front of the desk. She handed her the parchment. "Just dropping off the two copper vig for this bounty."

Regina's eyebrows rose and a smirk crossed her face when she saw the bounty. "Ahh, the missing person. Isn't that far below the Blades?"

"Change of scenery." She glanced around the room. "Is it safe to talk?"

Regina held up a finger. She opened a desk drawer and took out a gray sphere made of stone, which she set in the center of the desk. After a few seconds the stone began to glow purple and orange, as if it contained a fire inside. "No one can hear us now."

Saria's shoulders relaxed now that she could speak freely, or as freely as she ever would. She pulled the two death markers and a Skull Posse emblem and set them on the desk.

Regina's eyebrows rose at the sight. Her hands didn't move, though. "I'm sure there is a story here. I'm not sure I want to hear it."

Chaos Clan had been last seen three months ago attempting to take down a necromancer named Lady Calrur. The death marker the Blades had found when they fought off the Skull Posse was the only sign of them Saria had been able to find so far—and even that had been accidental. "It's about Talos."

Regina's expression tightened. "Tell me."

Saria launched into the story of the Skull Posse's attack in the woods, Gnedain's escape, and what they'd found in the pouch. The Mistress picked up the first of the death markers and held it out. The faces of Chaos Clan, including her son's, appeared over the marker. Tears welled in her eyes. "Do you know if they succeeded?"

"No, but I can't imagine the Skull Posse was strong enough to carry it out."

Regina picked up the second marker. Each of the Blades appeared, but Olive and Hilo's faces, who were no longer with the troop, were there with Saria, Ayre, and Perric's. "Well, that is a lovely drawing of Olive."

"I don't know if it helps us figure anything out, but this hit on the Blades must have been taken out before the troll bounty. Hilo is dead, and Olive is healing."

"Why would someone want your whole troop dead?"

That was a question Saria had been asking herself since their run-in with the Skull Posse. The Blades hadn't crossed anyone that she knew of, and Chaos Clan was strong enough to deter most assassins. "I have no idea, but it's a lead. If Chaos Clan were all dead, I think Skull Posse would have turned in the marker so they could get paid."

"True." Regina picked up the first marker and studied the drawing of Talos. "He was always taking risks. I always hoped he'd settle down, but the eldritch magic claimed him and that was it. I tried to talk them out of going after Lady Calrur. He'll fight until his dying breath."

Saria understood better than most. Talos and she had always been getting into some sort of trouble when they were growing up, going on epic adventures to raid the kitchen or steal from the guards. There was no risk too big for him. "Hopefully, he's still alive."

Regina set down the marker and pushed the pile toward Saria. "I have no right to ask, but would you keep your ears open for more news of him? Not as the Mistress, or your friend, but as a worried mother."

Saria would have done it without being asked, but her heart broke for her friend. It was easy to forget that they had been close before she'd taken on her job as the Mistress. "Of course, we will. Should we start by trying to find Lady Calrur?" Saria asked a bit reluctantly. The necromancer was rumored to be almost as powerful as the Nightmare Queen, she who opened the nexus portals to start the never-ending war.

"No, I don't want anyone to know you're looking for Talos. You should keep behaving as normal."

"Then we'll take this bounty. If we can get our coin for the Ashen Orb, the Blades will head out to track down this missing person."

"Brar wants to meet up with you here this evening at nine. She'll have your gold for you then."

"I'd rather you just get the gold from her and give it to us," Saria said. They'd done the job and she didn't trust Brar enough to want to give her any more opportunities to use the Blades.

Regina shrugged. "She has another offer for you and insisted on seeing you in person. She swears you'll find it quite profitable."

The last profitable bounty from Brar had almost killed her and her team. She didn't think she was interested in any more of the private jobs, regardless of who gave them. "I'll be here to get my gold. I'm not promising anything else."

———

S aria knocked on the door right before nine. She liked to be a bit early since you never knew what you'd discover when people weren't expecting you yet.

"Come in, Saria," Regina's voice came through the door.

Saria opened the stout wooden door and entered the dimly lit room. She closed the door behind her and headed for the closest guest seat but was both startled and displeased to find a person already occupied the high-backed chair.

"Hello, Saria. It's been a while," Brar Opalback said. The dwarven sorceress wore dark brown robes over cream-colored pants. Gems sparkled on a necklace and numerous rings. "The Blades did well retrieving the Ashen Orb."

Saria hid her reaction as best she could. "It almost killed us."

"But it didn't, so it shows I picked wisely," the sorceress said with a fake smile.

"Saria, take a seat," Regina said, gesturing to the empty chair on the left.

She thought about refusing but starting off a tense situation being stubborn wasn't going to make it any easier. After a moment, she took the proffered seat.

"Brar has another bounty she'd like the Blades to handle," Regina said.

Brar might pay well, but Saria didn't want to work with the sly sorceress again. "First, I need some information. What does the orb do?" Saria asked. "Why is it so important? The place was designed to keep anyone from getting it, and in my experience, there's usually good reason not to mess with an artifact that's got that many protections."

Brar laughed. "Always straight to the point, aren't you?"

"That doesn't answer my question."

Brar sighed. "Honestly, I don't know, but I know it is important."

"You send us on a suicide mission on the off-chance the orb could be useful? I don't buy it." Saria's cheeks heated with anger as she voiced her doubts. Magic users and priests always talked in double speak. They'd say anything to get what they wanted. Saria had little desire to deal with them and Brar more than most. The sorceress manipulated people like children played with dolls.

"Yet here you are," Brar said stiffly. "A seer saw the Ashen Orb while we were preparing to stop an invasion."

Brar had a bad reputation with the Duke Nalan of Whitecrest's staff. Brar had a bad reputation with everyone who knew her, in fact. The last Saria heard, Brar had been moved into of the royal residence in Whitecrest. Why would she care about an invasion? "Invasion? By who?"

"By monsters," Brar said grimly. "I understand that you are upset at being sent into a situation you weren't prepared for. If you allow me, I will explain the rest."

Saria fumed, but she nodded her assent. She hated the feeling she was being played. But if Brar's seer was right about another monster invasion, she at least owed her the time to listen.

Brar fiddled with her necklace for a moment before she began. "I hope you'll forgive me for starting so far in the past, but it will become apparent as the story unravels."

"Just get on with it."

"Saria," the Mistress said in her best mother's voice.

"Regina, don't worry. I know Saria well." Brar straightened in the chair which took a bit since her feet didn't reach the floor. "Before the Eylnian Empire fell, a stranger appeared on the continent of Montvern. She wore strange clothing, was barely alive, and didn't speak common or any of the known languages. After a time, she was taken in by the temple of Era'tal and healed. There she began her training."

"That was a hundred and fifty years ago. What does that have to do with the orb?" Saria asked, feeling a flood of annoyance. All she wanted was the promised gold and to be away from this place.

"Patience," Brar said. "She rose in the ranks, but it was discovered that she had made a pact with a demon. They banished her. She took on a title you might recognize. The Nightmare Queen."

Little was known of the woman who had begun the destruction on the empire, but Brar's information was plausible. That didn't mean she wasn't lying. "The one who caused the monster wars."

"Correct. Mistress Abernathy would be proud you listened in her classes," Brar said with a chuckle. "The Nightmare Queen opened all of the Nexus portals and brought creatures from across the dimensions to invade our world. I won't bore you with the history of the war, but the Queen began searching for the Ashen Orb during the battles. When I found a reference to the orb and the seer found the location, I asked you to retrieve it before the Queen could find it."

Saria held up a finger. "Wait. You're saying she's still alive? I figured she was long dead and anyone claiming to be her was a liar."

"True evil is immortal. Her powers have grown to the point where I do not believe I could best her."

Saria snorted. "Well, if she is, what's to stop her from taking it from you?"

"I'm hoping to turn its power against her. Which leads us to why I asked you here tonight, but first we need to settle up." Brar reached under her robe and produced five jingling pouches. She held them out to Saria.

Saria had never held this much money at once, but she'd had over a hundred silvers before. The bags were heavier than expected. Her brows knitted together in confusion.

"Each bag has two hundred gold pieces. I truly didn't know how taxing the bounty would be, but you delivered as I knew you would. This is but a token of my gratitude."

Brar's oily smile belied her words. No doubt she'd known just how dangerous the task was and had picked them because they were disposable if they failed. The real question was whether Brar and the Ashen Orb were linked to the assassinations. It didn't make sense she would be, since Chaos Clan had also had a marker and hadn't been attempting to retrieve that bounty, but it was more than Saria wanted to dig into. "The Blades thank you and I will bid you farewell. We have a bounty that we are leaving at first light."

"Yes, the missing person bounty," Brar said with a tone of condescension. "Will you be taking bounties to clean houses next?"

Saria bristled, standing to leave. "We'd clean houses, but

Ayre steals the silver. The Blades delivered your orb, and we are done with you. I'll be leaving now."

"Please sit, Saria," Regina said. "At least hear her request."

The pleading tone was not lost on Saria. The Mistress of Bounties never begged for anything. Saria sat back down, let the weight of the gold settle into her lap, and sighed. "Fine. Say your piece."

2

T hank you," Brar said. "I have need of an artifact that is stored in Ironhold."

"Ironhold? The dwarven capital?" Saria knew Brar was ambitious and ruthless at times, but the dwarves had kicked her out, and anyone who went against them was a fool. Stealing from them was insanity.

Brar smiled. "The very one. King Dotrul Greyshoulder has a staff in his armory that Gild Leatherbrow took into battle centuries ago. I need it to craft a weapon that will destroy the Nightmare Queen and close all the portals once and for all. With it I can bring peace to all of Providence."

Saria's mouth hung open. To refuse her request might put the Blades in danger, since Brar might take exception to being denied, but the danger was far less than attempting to break into the dwarven stronghold. Dwarves didn't take trespassing lightly. Dwarves didn't take *anything* lightly. They had survived the monster wars behind the stone walls of their kingdom, much like the elves sheltered in the massive Eternal Groves "You want the Blades to steal from the dwarven king in the middle of his impregnable fortress? You are insane."

"I will pay you each one thousand gold to fetch me the staff."

A thousand gold? They could buy armor and weapons to catapult them into the top rungs of the bounty board. They could truly help protect the people of Southern Holm.

"One thousand gold for a couple of weeks of your time. You'll be rich. I know the secret passages into the stronghold. A team can slip in and retrieve the item with minimal risk."

"We aren't interested." Saria stood. "I thank you for the gold. Find another band to do your dirty work."

"Dirty work?" Brar said, her voice rising. "I am trying to save the world."

What a load of shit. The Nightmare Queen probably wasn't alive, and she probably planned to use the Ashen Orb to get revenge on the dwarves for kicking her out or something equally petty and useless. The only thing Brar cared about was herself. "I don't give a fuck for the world," she lied. "I protect my troop first and foremost. If it is so easy, have the Violet Swarm or the Ice Tigers get it for you. Hell, go get it yourself."

"You know I've been banished. I'd be put to death for stepping foot inside Ironhold."

"As would the Blades if we were caught. No, Brar. I will not be your puppet." She turned to the Mistress. "The Blades will be leaving to find the missing person as per the bounty we took. Is that acceptable?"

Regina looked back and forth between the two. She cleared her throat. "As per the covenant, you are bound to perform the duties you have freely accepted. Go in peace."

"Thank you." She nodded to Brar. "Good eve, Brar. I hope when we meet again it is under more agreeable circumstances."

"How dare you turn me down," Brar said.

"Brar, she's under no obligation—" Regina started.

"You were a gutter rat when the Mistress brought you in for training. You know nothing of the world past the end of your sword. You think the scum you run with will accept that you turned down all that gold? No, they will slice your throat and accept my offer. As they should. How will you live with yourself knowing you allowed the world to die because you refused to assist me in saving it?"

If Brar was telling the truth about the seer…and the Nightmare Queen…

But no. Brar's only goal was power. Saria had seen her destroy good people whom she'd seen as threats. No, Brar wanted something other than saving the world.

"The world can burn and so can you." Saria stomped out of the office and went to the common room to find her troop. They sat in quiet conversation at a corner table. She stormed over to them. "Get your gear, we are leaving."

"What?" Perric asked. "We were headed over to the—"

"I don't care if you were planning to fuck twenty people all at once. We are leaving in ten minutes. Meet me out front. I'll explain on the way."

Ayre stood. "You heard her. Ten minutes."

The thief headed up the stairs to his room. Jileli and Lithia followed. Only Perric remained seated. Saria turned to leave.

"What is going on? This isn't like you," Perric said.

As much as she loved Perric, right now she could bang his head against a wall. They didn't have time to stand around parsing every detail. "We are in danger and need to go. I just pissed off a very powerful sorceress who is well known for taking revenge on people who disappoint her."

Perric downed his ale. "I will expect a full explanation."

"And you will have it." She turned and took the stairs two

at a time. Brar used people to her own ends, abandoned them when she tired of them, and destroyed any who crossed her.

Saria had just crossed her. While she wished Regina wouldn't have trusted the sorceress enough to work with her, she couldn't turn down bounties just because she, too, had a history with the individual. Though Brar had never targeted Regina like she had so many others.

Saria threw the door open to find Selwyn sitting on her bed. Of all the days for him to be intruding on her when she had to get out of town. "I don't have time for you."

"Regina sent me. I heard the whole thing. You have to leave town now. She is keeping Brar in her office, but the sorceress has called you a traitor and we both know her wrath is deadly."

"No shit. My troop is gathering their kits as we speak. I've had too many run-ins with Brar. The best way to deal with her is to vacate until she calms down." Saria moved to the end of the bed and grabbed her pack. The sword strapped around her waist in an instant and she shoved her arms into the pack straps.

"I guess you prepared for this?" Selwyn asked.

"I prepare for everything. If you'll excuse me, I'll be leaving now."

"Do you want the second part of the message?" Selwyn asked with that damn creepy smile.

Saria rounded on him. "I don't have time for your games or your off-color comments. Tell me whatever Regina wants me to know, or by Ylo's right hand I will gut you where you sit."

The Keeper of the Roles shrugged off the threat. He'd been one of the most powerful mages at one point, and she had no idea the extent of his abilities now. Perhaps they'd faded with age, so he'd decided to work as a bookkeeper and enchanter of markers. Whatever the reason he cut to the point. "The Mistress asked me to tell you the man you seek placed the bounty on himself. He wants whoever took the bounty to find him."

"What?" Saria asked, and it came out louder than she wanted. More quietly, she added, "Who does that?"

"I asked him, but he said that destiny would lead the correct troop to his doorstep. He set out for a small town called Coldbrook to the southeast of Auano. He told me he'd leave a clue there to his next destination," Selwyn said.

The last thing they needed was another mystery to solve. "Destiny? Is this guy a crackpot?"

"He was..." Selwyn said, rubbing his chin while he searched for the correct word. "Confused. Magi get like that sometimes."

"Not the good ones," Saria said with a laugh. The bounty directed them to Auano, which was four or five days away. Coldbrook was closer, a bit over three days but would take them to the east far enough to avoid Brar, the other troops, and anyone else who might be looking for them. Like assassins. "When they've dabbled in the occult for too long, they might lose their grasp on reality, I suppose. Regardless, it is the perfect excuse to get the Blades as far from Brar as possible. She'll cool down after a while."

Selwyn didn't look convinced. "I hope so. She was very angry that you turned down her 'generous' offer."

"After my troop almost died, she can find another stooge." Saria placed a hand on the door latch, but then stopped. "I need you to relay a message back to Regina. If I hear it from anyone else, I will kill you. Do you understand?"

He shook his head like a parent being threatened by a toddler. "I make extra gold on the side, but not by betraying Regina. You are safe to tell me."

She doubted it, but without another avenue, this was the

THE DRAGON'S WRATH BOUNTY

best she had. "I didn't have time alone with her, so you'll have to do."

"Such high praise."

"Let's get one thing straight," Saria said with a pointed glare at the Keeper. "I don't like or trust you. Why Regina hasn't fed you to the ravens is beyond me."

"Understood. What is the message?" Selwyn asked.

His eyes were downcast, and he looked upset, but Saria didn't have time to worry about it. "Tell Regina if I have to, I'll send information about Talos through someone else. I'll tell them to tell her what she said after I was promoted to guard captain."

"And what was it?" Selwyn asked.

"I'm not about to tell you," Saria said, "but Regina will know."

3

Saria was the first down to the bar. She slid her backpack under the table to reduce the number of patrons who saw it. There weren't a lot of people in the bar with the faire a week away, but the less people who saw them rush out of here the better.

Ayre strolled across the tavern with his rucksack slung over his shoulder. He appeared calm, but his hand didn't stray from his dagger. His eyes flickered around the room. He might have a strange sense of humor, as most elves did, but he was deadly in a fight.

Saria nodded to him, and he headed out into the night to wait for the rest. She wondered if she'd been hasty in turning down Brar, but the only place she wanted to break into less than Ironhold would be an elvish city. Not that anyone could find them with all the magic they employed to keep themselves hidden from the outside world. Elves like Ayre were rare in Southern Holm. Most of his people spent their long lives in the safety of their homeland.

Lithia came down next. The shadow fae ignored the

hostile glances from the few others who sat in the tavern. Her pale skin and red eyes made her stand out. Saria still didn't know why the archer had left the underground kingdom, but she was skillful with a bow and a fantastic cook. Without her, they would have all been dead.

Saria stood and followed Lithia out the front. A few minutes later, Perric and Jileli exited the building with their gear. Perric had a petulant grimace on his face. "We couldn't have left in the morning?'

"Feel free to stay the night at the Velvet Pearl, but the sorceress will be looking for someone to take her ire out on. I plan on being far from here. Selwyn was in my room to warn me to leave now before she finishes talking with the Mistress."

"This is serious," Jileli said with a meaningful look at the paladin. "We should be leaving."

"My thought exactly," a deep voice said from the shadows. Trollslayer stepped into the light that pooled under the lanterns that flanked the tavern's door. "The Mistress requested that we keep the gate open and for me to escort you. I don't know why, but I don't need to. Shall we?"

Saria started, but laughed when she saw him. "You are always showing up where I least expect you."

"The mayor pays my salary, but we all know who runs Moonbourne," he said with a wink. "Let's get you out of here before anything bad happens."

"I like that plan." Perric hoisted his backpack and gestured for Trollslayer to lead the way.

The huge guard captain escorted the Blades through the mostly deserted streets. The occasional harlot called out to the group and a few thieves vanished into the night as the party made their way to the gates. True to his word, the sally port stood open with two guards standing watch. They saluted as Trollslayer approached and then left without a word.

Trollslayer gestured to the passage. "Time for the Blades to fly." He laughed at his own joke.

Saria shook his hand. "Thank you. We will--"

Trollslayer held up his huge hand. "I don't want to know. I can't slip if I don't know."

"Wise man." Ayre patted the guard's arm and slid out the door. The others followed.

"Thank you, my friend," Saria said after Lithia cleared the gate. "We'll be back."

Trollslayer's face contorted into a scowl. "Take your time. Brar has a long memory for those who have wronged her, and she has eyes everywhere."

"She'll get over it," Saria said. "I've known her since I joined the Duke's personal guard. She might make things difficult for us, but it will pass."

He didn't look convinced. "Something has changed. Just watch your back."

Saria nodded and stepped through the gate. The door latched behind her. After a moment's hesitation, Saria collected the troop. "Perric, take the lead."

"Do we stay on the road, or should we try one of the forest paths?"

"We need to move fast. Take the road until we find a traveler's rest. We'll catch some sleep, then set out for Coldbrook in the morning."

"There is a safe house an hour or so from here where we can hole up in," Lithia said. "It's big enough for the five of us."

"You should lead then," Perric said to her.

She glanced at Saria, who nodded. "Lithia, lead on. We need to be out of sight as soon as possible."

The team trotted after Lithia, who set an aggressive pace.

The night was alive with the sounds of bugs and frogs as the troop increased their distance from Moonbourne. The farms and guarded pastures for livestock fell away as they entered the low-lying hills outside of the city's zone.

The road had ended with the farms, so now they pushed through the tall grass of the plains. Lithia followed a game trail if it could be called that. Rocks stubbed toes and tripped the unsuspecting as they trudged along.

"How much farther?" Ayre asked when they reached their third hour of walking. "You said it was only an hour away."

"Another fifteen minutes or so," Lithia said from the front of the line. They had entered a part of the grasslands that included some copses of trees and the occasional stream. "It should be on our right once we pass the obelisk."

Perric groaned. "There is no rest for the weary."

"You mean wicked," Ayre said with a laugh. "You're just upset that you aren't at the pearl with Avilya."

"Look who's talking," Perric said. "You'd have been with half the brothel by now."

"Jealous?"

"If you two are done, we are here," Lithia said. A small stone obelisk sat in the swaying grass. The archer left the path and uncovered a door set into the side of a hill. The woven grass mat blended in perfectly with its surroundings.

"How did you know this was here?" Jileli asked with a wondering tone.

"The shadow fae have small hiding holes all over Southern Holm. When your race is hunted, it is good to have a place to lie low while enemies are searching for you. It will keep anyone from finding us."

She placed her hand next to the door, and it swung open. Lithia doubled over and entered the safety of the cave.

Saria waved the rest to go in while she watched behind

them. No lights or sounds followed, but for a sorceress as strong as Brar, that didn't mean much. Once everyone was inside, she knelt and crawled through the door, pulling it shut behind her.

A long shaft had been dug deeper into the hillside. It took a bit to crawl along, but eventually it opened up into a good-sized cavern. Wooden boxes covered the back wall of the hideout. The room glowed faintly with numerous runes that had been etched into the stone.

Lithia cleared her throat when she realized the troop stared at the glowing glyphs. "They are for protection and to keep magic from spying on the place. Those who hunt the shadow fae have many methods beyond hounds and rumors."

"Good to know." Perric unbuckled his sword and got out his bedroll. "I assume we are leaving in the morning?"

Saria thought for a moment. "Lithia, is there another place like this near Coldbrook?"

"There is. It is a couple of hours outside the town. It will take three days to get there. I can guide us to other safe places. We can travel at night to avoid being seen."

"Are we in that much danger?" Jileli asked her leader.

"I'm not sure, but Trollslayer and Regina thought so. Better to be safe. We can wait out the day and get some rest. We leave an hour after nightfall."

"I could use the sleep," Ayre said, throwing his pack across from where Perric had set up. "It's been a long time since we've had a break."

"It has," Saria said. What she didn't say was that she was concerned. Brar was formidable and turning down a job she claimed any troop could do shouldn't have set her off to this degree. While Brar was mean and vindictive, now that Saria had had a couple long hours to contemplate it, Regina's message was more than a simple warning. It had to be. Brar could ask stronger troops to do this job, and most of them would at least try. Something else was up.

"Get some sleep and we'll plan in the morning."

Saria hoped the wards would protect them, because if Brar Opalback was after them, she wasn't sure she could protect her troop or herself.

4

Lithia nudged Saria. "It's morning. We've got company."

Saria sat and rubbed her eyes. The light in the cave hadn't changed since the troop had entered. "How can you tell?"

"She is tal'tha," a deep male voice said from the darkness of the tunnel. A pale-skinned warrior stepped into the dim light of the cave. He wore banded mail with a pelt attached to his shoulders that hung past his waist. A thick hunting blade was in his hand. "The question is why a krova is trespassing on our territory."

Lithia stiffened. Her hand moved to her belt knife. "I am Lithia, of the Nat'kran clan. My troop needed refuge from the night, so I brought them to the safety of the protejel."

"I am Kranthal of the Da'thel clan and the leader of my war band. Even the dogs of the Nat'kran clan know the rules. Outsiders are not allowed in the protejel. You have endangered our people by allowing them knowledge of our safe house," he said, then spat on the floor. "You sully yourself by traveling with the johur."

"Johur." Ayre placed his hand over his heart like he'd been wounded. "None of us are dirty or a half-breed."

"Well, I am," Jileli said with a smirk. Her horns glowed purple.

"Keep our sacred words out of your mouth, johur," Kranthal said, glaring at the thief. "You are the betrayers and should be wiped out to allow the tal'tha our rightful place."

Ayre stepped forward, but Lithia placed her hand on his arm. "I'll take care of this."

Kranthal gestured and four more shadow fae entered the lit portion of the cave. Each wore the same armor minus the cloak. They spread out to either side of Kranthal with their weapons drawn.

Lithia strode up to the leader and slapped him across the face. "You have cast shame on my clan, and I demand justice."

The shadow fae warrior's hand started to rise toward his reddening cheek, but he dropped it to the side. "What is to stop me from killing the lot of you? You are krova. Your clan won't even mourn your loss."

"I have chosen the warrior's path. I hunt the monsters that have invaded our world instead of cowering in the caves, waiting for the surface dwellers to fight our battles."

"I am no coward," Kranthal said, puffing up his chest like a prized rooster. "I have led our people against horrors you've never dreamed of. I will grant you Sha'ly to determine the fate of the johur you've sullied yourself with."

"What is Sha'ly?" Perric asked.

"It is ritual combat to determine who is right," Lithia said to Perric before turning back to Kranthal. "You will let my troop go and grant us access to the safe houses if I best you?"

"As long as they don't try to stop the fight," Kranthal said with a shrug. "They are trash, but if any dare interfere, they will die screaming. If you lose, they will be taken as slaves."

Lithia knew what she was doing, or at least Saria hoped

she did. The shadow fae were a mystery to her. Saria hadn't grown up inside a culture that forced her to follow archaic rules or customs. Maybe there was an upside to being an orphan. "We agree," Saria said.

"No one will interfere in our fight," Lithia confirmed.

"Let us begin." Kranthal and his people retreated into the tunnel.

"Lithia, are you sure about this?" Saria asked when the shadow fae had departed. "We are stronger than they are."

The archer shook her head. "Kranthal will have sent a runner to get more warriors since we are in the Da'thel clan's area. If I don't best him, they will hunt us."

"I have a couple of tricks up my sleeve if needed," Ayre said with a wicked grin. "I'd love to shove my dagger into that bastard."

"Ayre, stay out of it," Jileli said.

"I don't like this," Perric said with a huff. "We could take them."

"And if we do, can we guarantee we won't be overrun by the rest of the clan's warriors?" Saria had given her word to the haughty fae, and there was no going back now. "No, this is Lithia's fight."

Perric caught her eye, and she dropped her chin in answer. If Lithia lost the combat, obviously the Blades would fight back rather than acquiesce to being enslaved or killed.

They followed Lithia out of the cave and into the early morning sun. The trees cast enough shade so no one was blinded as they emerged from the dark. The shadow fae had tramped down a circle in the dirt and grass as a makeshift battle arena.

Lithia pulled her knife and stood across from Kranthal. He had taken off his cloak and ran an oilskin cloth over the blade. His eyes bored into Lithia as she readied herself. The male shadow fae was larger and stronger, but Lithia fought like a demon. The overconfident sneer on Kranthal's face would soon be removed.

One of the others stepped between them. He had a scar from his right ear down to his chin. He raised his hands in front of each of the combatants. "I am Zan of the Da'thel clan. We fight by the rules of the Sha'ly. The fight is to the death." He turned to Lithia. "As per the law, do you have a second to bury you?"

To the death? Lithia had conveniently left that part out. Saria cleared her throat. "I will second her."

"Good. I will second Kranthal. If he falls, I shall assume his place as the leader." At that, Kranthal scowled. "Any who enter the ring will forfeit their life," Zan continued, looking at the Blades where they stood behind the archer. "Any breaking of the rules on either side calls for immediate execution."

Saria caught a faint eagerness on Zan's face. Could he be wanting Lithia to win? Were Kranthal and Zan rivals? This could get interesting depending on how the fight went.

Two of the shadow fae hefted their bows to show themselves ready. In unison, they said, "We will uphold the tal'tha customs. We are one with the darkness."

Without another word, Zan strode from the circle. Once outside it, he nodded. "May Ylo welcome the loser into their kingdom. Fight."

Kranthal lunged at Lithia, who sidestepped his initial attack. She slashed at his head, but it fell short of the mark. They circled each other, feinting and jabbing to test the other's skills.

"You fight well for a krova. Usually, the clan sells outcasts as slaves," Kranthal said before launching another attack meant to catch Lithia in the throat.

The archer spun under the blow. Her dagger flickered

and a string of blood from Kranthal's thigh flew across the ground. She followed it up with a reverse attack.

The warrior jumped back out of range, but his knife scored a small cut on Lithia's exposed forearm. He grinned at her like he knew a joke no one else knew.

Lithia backed up and reset her stance.

Saria noted the archer had fallen for a false opening in his defenses. She was lucky he barely broke the skin on his riposte.

"Your weapon master should be flogged if that is the best they taught you," Lithia said. Her forehead beaded with sweat even though the day was cool and the fight barely begun.

"My master taught me well," Kranthal said with a smirk. "Not everything in a fight is blade work."

They began to circle again. Lithia stumbled, but recovered before the warrior could close on her. She dodged to the left, then delivered a slash that caught her opponent across the bicep. He grunted and stabbed back, but Lithia had fallen into the crushed grass. She rolled and got to one knee.

"You are weak," Kranthal said to her as he paced outside of her knife range. "Give up now and I will allow you to serve me."

"I am not a whore," Lithia said, eyes blazing. She pushed herself to her feet. The archer wobbled as she stood.

"Lithia, are you good?" Saria asked. The archer swayed slightly, not her usual, energetic self. Was she faking?

"I am," she said through gritted teeth. "I will end this now."

Kranthal laughed. "The only thing you will do is die."

The archer lunged, but tripped, falling face first. She landed with a hard thud on the ground. Jileli started towards her fallen companion. but Saria held her back.

"We can't interfere," Saria said, loud enough for all to hear. She'd kill that trumped up jackal if he killed Lithia, but she didn't know if this was part of an elaborate plan by Lithia to lure in Kranthal. "Let her finish the fight."

Jileli tried to pull free from Saria's grip but failed. "There is something wrong. Look at her arm."

The skin around the scratch from Kranthal's dagger had turned black. So. Not faking. "Poison."

"Yes," Ayre said, moving to stand next to Saria. "He must have coated his blade before the fight."

"Is that allowed in a battle like this? Why wouldn't Lithia have been using poisons when she fought with us?" Saria asked. She glanced at Zan, but the second in command started intently at the battle.

Kranthal stood over the fallen archer. "You aren't even worth keeping alive for sport." He flipped her on to her back so she faced him.

Lithia mumbled something, but it came out as a garbled mess. She tried to lift her head, but it crashed back to the ground.

"I will send your friends to join you in the afterlife," Kranthal said.

Saria braced herself to watch Lithia die.

5

Kranthal raised his blade, prepared to strike down Lithia where she sprawled on the ground. Green tinged bubbles flowed out of her mouth as she tried to speak.

Before the blade could fall, Kranthal was stopped. Forcibly. Zan had broken his own commandment and entered the circle where he held a blade to their leader's neck.

"Hold," Zan ordered. "Check her."

Another warrior strode over and knelt before Lithia. Her head lolled to the side. Green drool trickled from her mouth. He lifted her face and smelled her breath. "She's been poisoned with jeath."

"That's what I thought," Zan said. He reached around and took Kranthal's knife from him.

"Are you accusing me of violating the solemn oath I took?" Kranthal said in a snotty tone. "She's not worthy of dying a painless death from jeath."

Zan smelled the dagger and recoiled. He dragged the knife across his leader's exposed arm. Blood welled up from the cut. "We'll see if you are telling the truth, Kranthal. Give her the antidote."

The warrior knelt beside Lithia pulled a vial from his belt pouch and forced it into her mouth, holding her nose until she swallowed it. "It will take a while, but she'll recover."

Zan lowered his blade and stepped back.

Kranthal sneered at all of them. "Look. I am fine. There was no poison on my blade."

Zan laughed. "A liar to the very end."

"I demand justice," Kranthal said. He advanced on Zan but stumbled. "You have no right."

"If your word were true," Zan said calmly, "you wouldn't be slurring or off balance."

Kranthal retrieved a small vial from his belt pouch like the one they had given Lithia. Zan slapped it out of his hand and drove his dagger into the other man's chest. "Justice has been served. You are a failure as a leader and have sullied our reputation by breaking our sacred code."

Kranthal's hands shook as they tried to pull the knife from his chest. He failed and slumped to the ground. Zan kicked him over and spit on his former leader.

Saria ran to check on Lithia, who had remained unmoving after being force-fed the antidote. She snored softly, but no more green saliva dripped from her mouth. "You aren't allowed to use poison against each other, I take it?"

Zan nodded. "Kranthal's knife had enough to slow her so he could kill her, but to use it against other shadow fae is shameful. You have my oath as the war band leader of the Da'thel that she will be fine, and I offer our hospitality to stay until she recovers. Our people will not harm you or yours."

Ayre nodded to Zan. "We accept your generous offer and will bind our hands if we ever cross paths again. May we leave as friends?"

Zan's features stilled. Elves and the shadow fae, for all their similarities, hated each other. After a long pause, Zan spoke. "Our people have been enemies for many eons, but it would do us all well to put those feelings aside, given the invasion of our lands. I cannot speak for the tal'tha, but you have nothing to fear from my clan."

"We thank you for your honorable treatment." Ayre sketched a bow Saria had never seen before.

"How do you know our ways?" Zan said. His eyes were as wide as soup bowls.

"I spent time with your people as a child," Ayre said with a shrug. "It is a story for another time over a few pints of ale."

"I'd like to hear that story." Jileli laughed. "You are full of surprises, Ayre."

"That's not the only thing he's full of," muttered Perric.

Ayre ignored him.

Saria changed the subject. "We should get Lithia back inside to rest. Will you join us?"

Zan shook his head. "We are duty bound to return the traitor's corpse to our people."

"What kind of threat would coax the tal'tha from their underground cities?" Saria asked with a frown. "Lithia is the first of your people I've seen in years. And now you."

"We do not know," Zan shook his head. "The elders have sent all the war bands out to investigate. The omens point to destruction, but they are unclear."

"Interesting timing." Ayre spun his dagger through his finger. "Do you think—"

Saria stopped him. "Ayre! Zan needs to return Kranthal's body to their people. We are wasting their time."

Zan bowed to Saria. "Thank you. While we can live in the sun, it isn't our preference. May Gartog protect you and yours. Until our paths cross again."

Saria returned the bow. "Thank you, Zan. May Gartog protect you in your travels."

The shadow fae warrior barked orders in their tongue. Within moments, they had trussed up their dead leader and set off at a trot.

Saria watched them go. "Let's get Lithia inside so she can recover."

Perric scooped the archer up and carried her back to the safe house. Jileli ran ahead and opened the hidden door.

Saria put her hand on Ayre's arm. "We don't want to talk about the orb or Brar or any of the rubbish she told me." Saria had told the team about Brar's insane plans. None of them valued gold over their lives. "If there is a connection between the orb and whatever the shadow fae read in their omens, we don't want that kind of attention."

"Saria, it's only been a day since we left Moonbourne. I doubt the orb has anything to do with what Zan was talking about. For all their formal speech and 'refined' ways, the shadow fae are superstitious to a fault. One time the shadow fae abandoned an underground settlement because of a bad omen. A few years later they returned, and nothing had happened."

"I don't like the timing."

"I understand, but I've lived a lot longer than you and have seen a lot of things," Ayre said. He frowned for a moment. "I will guard my words, though. If you are right, we could be in danger."

"After all, someone wants to assassinate us," she reminded him. "When do you think Lithia will recover?"

"Jeath is deadly in large amounts, but a simple cut will heal. We will probably need to lie low for a few days to let her rest," Ayre said. "The aftereffects are mostly being tired, and it's not like we are on an important bounty."

"All bounties are important."

"Most people think dragon dung can be used to brew love potions. I stopped worrying about other people's stupidity."

"You're an ass." Saria laughed. "Dragons have been gone for as long as I've been alive. No dragons, no dragon poop."

Ayre shrugged. "Doesn't mean I'm wrong."

He wasn't wrong.

6

Lithia slept off and on for the next four days with the Blades taking turns watching her. At last, on the fourth day, she sat up and glanced around. "What happened?"

"I told you to ease off the fungus ale," Ayre said with a laugh. "That stuff will kill you."

"I don't remember drinking." Lithia rubbed her eyes before noticing the cut on her arm. "How did I get cut?"

"Well, it started with this ogre challenging you to a drinking competition—"

"Ayre, don't be an ass," Saria said, going over to sit next to Lithia.

"Too late," Perric and Jileli said at the same time.

Saria explained the situation to the archer.

Perric brought over a small platter of food. Lithia picked at it for a moment before digging in. She listened while stuffing food into her mouth. Jileli handed her a mug of water, which she drained.

"More please," Lithia said, handing the mug back to the mage.

"Of course."

"What happened to Kranthal?" Lithia asked between bites.

"Dead. Zan killed him for breaking the rules of the ritual combat," Saria said.

Jileli passed over another mug of water. The blood mage took a seat next to Saria.

"Thank you." Lithia drained half in one swallow. "Serves him right. The sacred texts are very strict when there is combat among our people."

"You fought him," Perric said with an approving smile. "He could cheat or die."

Lithia's face was one of shock. Perric was a strong man who rarely praised anyone other than himself. "Thank you."

"No need for thanks," Perric said with a smirk. "You kicked his ass. You'll make a great Blade."

Saria quickly closed her slack jaw. "He's right. You fought like a demon."

"Hey," Jileli said. "I have feelings."

They all laughed.

Saria smiled. After all the fights and near-death experiences they'd shared, the Blades were pulling together as a team. No, a family. While she would miss Olive, Lithia and Jileli were meshing with the original three even better than she could have hoped.

And it was just as well they had become cohesive. If the shadow fae were to be believed, the time ahead would be treacherous. Added to the other news Saria had heard, she didn't think they were wrong.

"If we are going to cash in this bounty, we need to move as soon as Lithia is ready," Saria said. Lithia could probably use a few more days of rest, but they were too close to Moonbourne and Brar to give her much peace of mind. Frankly, she'd be happier to board a ship and head to

Montvern. With the Angry Sea between them, she might feel safe.

Jileli approached with a small bag in her hand. She knelt next to Lithia and pulled a small seed from the pouch. "Eat this."

The archer looked wary. "What is it?"

"It is an opi seed. It will help with your recovery and relieve any pain or fatigue from being poisoned."

Lithia took the seed, and after a moment, popped into her mouth and chewed. She made a face. "Tastes like stale vomit."

"If it tasted good, everyone would want them," Jileli said with a smile.

Jileli always surprised Saria. She'd been born from a demon beguiling her elven mother, but other than the horns and her magic, she was a kind soul. Well, until you pissed her off. The image of a Skull Posse attacker dissolving into a bloody puddle crept into Saria's mind. She pushed it away.

"If we leave today and push ourselves," Perric said, "we can make it to Coldbrook in two days."

"Always chasing something," Ayre said with a chuckle. "Gold, glory, or girls, it's all about the conquest."

"Not all of us chase anything that moves." Perric lifted his pack from the floor and threw it over his shoulder. "Not all of us have centuries to meander around, either."

"Ah, yes. I forget humans have limitations."

Perric's hand settled on his sword. "Elves forget they can die. You might want to consider that before you run your mouth."

Ayre's eyebrows shot up. "Why, Perric, are you threatening me?"

"No, my friend," Perric said with a shrug. "Just a reminder that your mouth almost killed us in the temple. Maybe curbing your tongue might be a good idea."

"If you two want to pull your dicks out to see whose is

bigger, can you do it outside? Lithia needs a few minutes to get ready to travel," Saria said. Four inactive days in the cave had set all their nerves on edge. For everyone's sake, she hoped the shadow fae was ready for the journey.

"No worries, my leader," Ayre said with a flourish. "We will await you outside."

Ayre strolled out of the room. Perric grunted, but followed.

"Are they always like that?" Lithia asked as she finished her food. "They act like pubescent boys."

"Men never really grow up," Jileli said from where she packed her kit. "They get bigger, not smarter. Ayre has had a century to grow out of it and you see how he is."

"Annoying?" Saria said with a laugh. She stood and helped Lithia to her feet.

The archer's face paled. With her light gray coloring, that was saying something. She straightened and looked Saria in the face. "I'll be all right."

Saria studied her for a moment. "If you need to rest, call out. I don't need you dropping on the trail."

"Just need to get used to standing again."

The three women left the cave to join the others outside. The day was overcast, and Saria smelled rain on the air. A good soaking would cover their tracks but made for miserable travel. Zan's warning echoed in her mind. What could be so horrible that the shadow fae would leave their underground cities to seek out the source? They surely hadn't done it for the monster invasion.

Saria slung her backpack over her shoulder. "We need to keep moving. We'll follow the road. If we push, we can sleep in a real bed tomorrow night."

"Down!" Perric yelled. The big man dropped to the ground. The others did the same, crouching in the tall, concealing grass.

Head level with the top of the weeds, Saria looked around for any signs of danger. "Perric?"

"Quiet," he snapped. His eyes searched the skies above.

"While I don't mind rolling in the dirt..." Ayre started, but fell silent. His eyes widened in fear. "By Era'tal's basket. What is that?"

Saria jerked her head around to where Ayre stared. Her mouth fell open in shock.

"Is that what I think it is?" Jileli asked in hushed tones.

Saria nodded. "That's a dragon."

An enormous beast soared below the clouds. The extended wings were larger than many taverns they'd stayed in. Its red scales glistened in the dim light. It roared, and Saria thought she might shit her pants. The wings beat down and the creature banked into a large, lazy circle. It reminded Saria of vultures circling the dying.

"We haven't seen a dragon since before the Eylnian Empire fell," Ayre said from where he laid flat on the ground. She could make him out between the stalks and grasses. "That thing is huge."

Another roar echoed through the still morning as the beast swung in a wide loop. Its head swung back and forth, appearing to search for something or someone on the ground. "Let's retreat to the cave. Be ready to move on my signal."

"I'll stay and keep watch," Ayre said. "I can blend in better than any of you. It won't spot me."

"Be careful," Saria said to the thief.

"I'm always careful," Ayre responded.

"Why is it here?" Jileli asked, her eyes fastened to the

dragon as it soared above them. "It is as beautiful as it is terrible."

Without warning, the dragon's head lifted, and it shot a column of flames across the sky.

"Move," Saria said in a low voice. The troop leapt into action. Perric reached the door to the safe house first and threw it open for the others. They pulled the door shut behind them, leaving Ayre to stand watch outside.

"Will he be safe?" Lithia asked when they had returned to the main part of the cave. The shadow fae slumped next to a crate and rested her back against the stone wall. Deep circles still bordered the archer's eyes.

"Ayre would give the dragon an upset stomach, so I think he'll be fine," Perric said with a forced laugh.

Saria's eyebrows rose. Obviously, the paladin was worried about Ayre. "He'll be fine. Ayre can conceal his presence better than anyone I've ever met."

Jileli sat on the floor with her belt pouches open. She took each vial out, inspected it, and returned it to its place. The blood mage had completely reorganized her stash while Lithia was out cold. Jileli's nerves must be getting the better of her.

Lithia, for her part, examined her arrows. The mithral arrow from the tomb had been set aside while she checked each arrow's tip and fletching. A second quiver of arrows lay next to her leg. Archers weren't overly useful without ammunition.

Saria sat, her back against the wall and her sword across her knees. It was an exercise they used in the Duke's guard to center yourself. A dragon. Why now of all times? Did it have something to do with the Ashen Orb? Or Brar? The sorceress was powerful, but she'd never heard of anyone summoning a dragon. The legends were quite clear that dragons were the apex predators, and now it was hunting over Southern Holm.

Twenty minutes passed in silence before Ayre called from the doorway. "Coast is clear. We should go now."

Saria tossed her rucksack over her shoulder and headed out of the cave. The others retrieved their belongings and followed.

Ayre's eyes were still on the sky. "I think we should head due west and use the Eternal Groves as cover. We can make our way north to Coldbrook from there."

"It will take us a couple of extra days," Perric grumbled as he joined them. "It will take two days if we follow the road."

Saria considered both options. If Ayre was nervous, then she'd listen to him. "The forest it is."

"Saria," Perric started, but when her eyes locked on his, he dropped his gaze. "With the lizard flying about, I guess it doesn't hurt to be careful. I just don't understand how there is a dragon after all this time."

"I thought they were extinct after the wars. Without a dragon stone or other powerful magic, we don't stand a chance against a red dragon," Jileli said. She glanced around the group. "The fae remember what it was like when the dragons emerged from the Spell Plains and the Malachite Desert looking for gold. Even without the rest of the monster horde, they laid waste to half the empire."

Perric scoffed. "That was over a hundred years ago."

"I was an apprentice to a hunter back then," Lithia said with a slow nod. That would make her older than Ayre by quite a bit, though elves measured age differently than humans like her and Perric. "He died in the first siege of D'Athra after a minotaur crushed his skull with a sledge."

Ayre sighed. "I was in Yllle Serinis when the monsters flooded our world. If the magi and wizards and such hadn't banded together to hide the city, it would have fallen and been erased from history."

Jileli remained silent. Her eyes looked haunted by whatever she considered.

Saria put her hand on the mage's shoulder. "We all live with horrors in our past and avoiding that dragon should keep that particular horror out of our future. It's settled. We head for the Eternal Groves, then Coldbrook. The forest offers better concealment than the road through the foothills," Saria said. Her gaze flickered up to make sure the sky remained clear.

"It's two or three days to the edge of the woods," Ayre said. "Two days to the river, then north to Coldbrook."

"Aren't you worried the missing person will be harder to find?" Lithia asked.

Saria shrugged. "While it would be great to find…" She retrieved the bounty parchment, unfolded the paper, and read it. "Ah, Elladon Kane. According to the description, he was a merchant who went missing coming back from Cloni on the western shores of Southern Holm. In reality, he set up this bounty himself, so I doubt we're on a deadline."

Perric whistled through his teeth. "Glad we aren't going to Cloni. That trip would take over a month under good circumstances."

"Since he said he'd leave a more instructions in Coldbrook, that's where we'll head," Saria said, while putting away the bounty. "The original reason was to get out of Moonbourne and away from Brar. Nothing's changed by the appearance of the dragon other than the course we take."

"Who sets up a bounty on themselves? Doesn't make much sense," Ayre said with a twist of his lips. "I'm not sure I like the sound of that."

"I guess we could have taken Brar's job to break into Ironhold to steal a rod. Does that sound better?"

Ayre's shocked look almost made Saria laugh. Dwarves and elves hated each other on the best of days.

"Like I said, anything that keeps me away from those grubby earthworms is good for me," Ayre said.

"I agree with Ayre," Jileli and Lithia said at the same time.

"Without a written invitation, I'm not stepping foot into the dwarven halls," Perric said.

"Let's get started," Saria said. "Ayre, take point and keep your eyes open for any dragon droppings."

The others glanced up into the cloudy sky.

It was going to be a stressful trip to Coldbrook.

8

C ould it rain any harder?" Ayre asked as the Blades crested a hilltop after three days of trudging through the inclement weather. "I swear my balls are turning into prunes in my breeches."

In the distance, a ragged tree line formed a barrier to the rolling grasslands they'd been hiking through. A scattered single tree here or there was the only sign of the forest trying to advance into the grasslands.

"Let's get into the woods and we can try to find some shelter." Saria sort of wished they'd picked the road after trekking over game trails, through the tall, wet grass, and cold camps at night. Her skin held the pucker of a decaying corpse. *Will I ever be dry again?*

"I need a long, hot bath," Jileli said from where she walked next to Saria.

"Forget the bath," Perric said with a laugh. "I want a warm bed."

"You'll want to wash before you find your warm bed. The stench of you would scare off even the most desperate whore," Lithia said in a playful tone.

Perric scoffed. "You're spending too much time with Ayre."

"No, I've been downwind of you for the past few hours."

Saria tensed until the big man laughed. "I'm a bit ripe. Welcome to the club."

Lithia's mouth dropped open for a moment before she composed herself. "Um... Thanks."

Perric could be mercurial at times, others downright stubborn, but always loyal. If Lithia had proved herself to the paladin, things would be easier. With a quick glance over her shoulder, she spotted the smile on his face. She doubted the jovial attitude would last, but she'd take it while it was there.

"Saria, could we have a word?" Ayre called from the lead. "If I'm not interrupting anything important."

Saria sped up, leaving Jileli to join the thief. Tangles of grass attempted to snatch her feet, but she pushed through. With her long legs, she caught up to him quickly. She matched his pace. A couple hundred feet ahead, the edge of The Eternal Grove spread out before them. The tall grass of the foothills transitioned into the scrub line of bushes and saplings. Behind it, towering trees formed a wall, but more importantly, a canopy to lessen the rain. Saria had hoped for more safe houses, but the shadow fae stayed well away from the forests of the elves.

"What is it, Ayre?"

He shot her a sidelong glance. "I can't be sure," he said, keeping his tone soft so his words didn't travel. "But I think we have company up ahead."

Saria stopped her head from jerking up. She turned to face Ayre. In a loud voice she said, "I don't care if your feet are tired, we go until I say stop."

Ayre pivoted toward her in mock anger toward her so she could look over his shoulder without being obvious. "We don't get a say now?"

Her eyes raced over the thick growth at the edge of the woods. She didn't see anything, but Ayre had much sharper eyes than she did. She opened her mouth to respond when a movement caught her eye. The foliage all bobbed under the rain, but a big branch shook in an odd way.

Ayre cleared his throat.

"Sorry. I think you're right." Saria lifted her voice. Given their location it could be anything from trolls to killer rabbits. If the assassins or Brar had tracked them, and they could be found this easily, they were as good as dead. "Fine, we stop at the edge of the woods for tonight."

"Excellent choice," Ayre said loudly.

Saria winked at him, then turned to gather the rest. She placed her hand flat against her stomach and with her thumb tucked under. Perric and Jileli nodded slightly. Lithia looked around, confused. She didn't know the sign. Troops tended to create their own battle signs so nobody else would have an advantage over them in a fight, and Lithia and Jileli hadn't had time to learn all of the Blades' signals.

"Ayre is right," Saria said, so her voice carried. "We will stop at the edge of the forest since we are all exhausted."

Lithia opened her mouth, but Perric cut her off. "I agree with Ayre. We really need to rest with all the injuries we've had."

"I don't think I could have gone much further," Jileli said.

"Lithia, do you want to help Ayre scout out a good campsite?" Saria asked. With two fingers, she made a chopping motion, hidden from the forest, a signal for where to attack. Lithia nodded.

"Sure thing." She ran ahead to join Ayre, who stood, arms crossed like a peevish child.

"Perric, take the right flank. I'll take left." She followed Lithia, subtly loosening her sword in the sheath as she pretended to limp. Perric's big blade still hung on his back.

Jileli's fingers flexed. They paced themselves so they were ten feet behind the leaders.

When Ayre and Lithia reached the edge of the forest, all hell broke loose. Bodies erupted from the shrubs and bramble. If not for Ayre's warning, they would have been caught unaware.

Distinctive, high-pitched laughs flooded the air. Gnolls! Harder to kill than kobolds but at least it wasn't a dragon.

Saria pulled her knife and sword free and whirled to face the closest monster. The monster stood well over a foot taller than Saria and wielded a clumsy looking spiked mace. Its spotted torso was bare, but it wore patchwork leather pants.

The first wild swing went wide. The gnolls cackled in that eerie pitch while they fought. Saria dodged the second swing and slid under the third. She stepped in and slashed across the stomach of the beast. Blood sprayed across the ground, but it was superficial at best.

Lithia's bowstring twang multiple times, followed by bestial screams of pain.

Another vicious stroke almost took Saria's head off. Behind her, her troop fought the rest of the pack. She caught the handle of the mace between her blades and attempted to kick the beast in the knee. Instead, her left foot slid out from under her on the wet grass and she hit the ground. The air exploded from her lungs and stars blanketed her vision.

The gnoll bayed in victory, standing over her. It gripped its weapon in both hands and pulled back to end her. Saria lashed out with her sword and struck her attacker's leg, throwing it off balance. The second it stumbled to the side, she rolled to her feet.

With a snarl, the gnoll charged her. She tried to pivot out of the way, but the gnoll was huge and far faster than she believed possible. Its shoulder caught her side and drove her to the ground yet again. Her sword flew from her hand to bury itself point first in the wet soil.

The gnoll crashed to the ground at the same time as her, the world tumbling around as they rolled to a stop. The barbs of the mace sliced across her bicep. Luckily, the gnoll hadn't landed directly on her or she'd have been pinned.

Saria used her free foot to push against the gnoll's legs, trying to unwrap herself, but it was too heavy. Its head whipped around and it tried to sink its teeth into her arm. She threw herself out of range of the muzzle, full of fangs.

The beast wiggled to the side to get more leverage, but the movement freed Saria's trapped leg in the process. She spun onto her back, avoiding the attack. It pounced on her, trying to bite her face in the process. The creature hadn't counted on the dagger that now protruded from its right eye. It snapped feebly as it died.

Saria pushed to her left, dislodging the corpse. She yanked her dagger free and peered around. The Blades had killed eight gnolls, though from the reservoir of goo in front of Ayre and Lithia, the number could be higher.

"Is everyone okay?" Saria asked her team.

"Just a minor cut here," Perric said. "Looks like you drew the biggest brute. Tough fighters for sure."

"It took everything I had to drop that one," Saria said, gesturing at the dead gnoll on the ground behind her. "Can you patch up your wound or do you need help?"

Perric's eyes slid to Jileli, and he frowned. "I'll handle it."

Jileli opened her mouth to respond, but never got the chance.

A loud bark silenced the area. A moment later, the largest gnoll she had ever seen burst into the open.

"Watch out!" Saria shouted.

9

The massive, armored gnoll crashed into the Blades, sending Ayre, Lithia, and Jileli flying from the impact. Perric pivoted and slashed across the shoulder of the beast with his sword, but the monster brushed past him.

Saria was keenly aware her sword had flown into the grass. Her dagger didn't appear up to the job of slaying this monstrosity, but the lives of her troop depended on her and Perric.

The monster reared back its enormous head and howled. It held a huge battle ax in one hand and boasted pieces of rusted plate mail over its shoulders and knees. A string of skulls were fastened into a belt around its waist.

Perric was the first to respond. He came in from behind it and attempted to hamstring the beast, but the giant gnoll blurred into motion. The crescent shaped ax arched around and knocked Perric's sword away with a great clang.

Saria switched her grip on her dagger and drove it into the exposed arm of their attacker. The knife bit deep, but it flew free when the gnoll jerked away. It howled in pain but didn't stop fighting. The flat of its blade struck Saria, throwing her backward.

"Come on, scavenger. I will teach you not to attack your betters." Perric advanced on the gnoll who danced to the side, keeping both Perric and Saria in its sights.

Saria pushed herself to her feet, grateful that the blade hadn't sliced her in half, though she'd be covered in bruises under her leathers. The spiked mace from the gnoll she'd killed was close at hand, so she grabbed it. The balance was off, but it was better than fighting bare handed.

The beast howled again. The sound set every hair on Saria's body on edge.

Perric moved to his right, and Saria slid to the left. This way they wouldn't accidentally hit each other and kept the gnoll from being able to focus in one place.

Saria feinted in, jabbing the mace like a spear. The gnoll tried to parry with the ax, but Saria had already retreated.

Perric swung his two-handed sword and caught the beast behind the left knee. Sparks flew from where the sword cleaved into the old plate, but it held. Perric brought the sword up and blocked a counter. The once silent clearing now sounded more like a smithy, with all the clanging steel.

Froth poured from the mouth of the gnoll. It snorted, sending a shower of snot out in front of it. It swung its ax in front of it a couple of times, watching Perric and Saria as they danced into position.

"What's the play?" Perric asked. His sword was at the ready.

"Saria," Lithia's voice came from behind them where she'd landed. "Jileli is hurt. She's bleeding badly."

"Stop the bleeding. We'll finish this." Saria caught Perric's eye. "High, low."

He nodded. Saria counted to three in her head. She screamed, drawing the gnoll's attention. It hefted the ax and ran toward her. She slammed the mace up to strike the gnoll's muzzle and missed.

Perric swung his sword to take out the monster's legs. The blade bit into flesh, sending a spray of blood across the ground. The gnoll pivoted, knocking the mace down. It leapt across and landed on Perric, claws raking the paladin's armor.

"I can't stop the bleeding," Lithia screamed, hysteria creeping into her voice.

Emotions warred in Saria's mind. She couldn't leave Perric, but Jileli could be dying. Save the living and mourn later, Regina's voice came to her from the years spent training in the Duke's guard. She spotted her dagger sticking out of the ground by where the gnoll and Perric struggled.

"I need help."

She ignored the archer's pleas. Instead, she ran, snatching the dagger. She jumped onto the back of the gnoll. She slammed the dagger down, intending to slice into the exposed neck, but it bounced off the armor.

The gnoll reared, shaking like a dog to dislodge Saria. It bucked and snarled as it fought to free itself.

Saria's grip slipped, and she fell to the ground, but she kept her balance and jumped again, landing squarely on the monster's back. The gnoll's head smashed into Saria's face. Her nose crunched, and blood flowed from the hit. Her vision blurred from the tears that rushed into them.

The beast threw itself back, but Saria held on for her life. If she fell, it would be over for her. Words came unbidden to her mouth. A strange snarling language erupted in a series of noises. With a primal scream, she drove the dagger into the back of the gnoll's head. It pitched forward, throwing Saria free in the process.

"Get this fucking thing off me," Perric said from under the dead gnoll.

Saria pulled Perric free and ran to where Jileli lay in the grass with Lithia using a cloak to try to stop the bleeding. The archer's forehead had a nasty gash across it. Ayre lay off to the side, but the thief's groaning indicated he was more stunned than injured.

"Perric," Saria yelled. "Help her."

Perric carefully pulled back the cloth and gasped. An open wound ran from hip to hip just under her belly button. Blood boiled out as the pressure from the makeshift bandage released. "This is bad."

"We need you to heal her or she'll be dead in minutes."

Perric shook his head. "I don't think holy rites will work on her. She's half demon and I could hurt her more than I could help."

"I don't fucking care," Saria said. The harshness of her voice shocked even herself, but Perric looked like he'd been slapped. "What does it matter if she bleeds out or dies because you are trying to help?"

"It matters to me," he said in a soft tone. "I don't want to hurt her."

"Shut the fuck up and do something," Saria said in a tone sharp enough to cut metal. "You've healed worse."

"And if she dies?"

"She's already dead if we can't help her."

"I'll try my best," Perric said softly. "Oh, Lady Drohara, please help me in our time of need."

Saria held her breath, waiting for a miracle that might not come.

10

Perric bowed his head and placed his hands on either side of the wound in Jileli's abdomen. His words were low but forceful. His eyes were closed and his hands softly glowed. The glow intensified from a soft gold to an angry red.

Jileli bucked, screaming like she was being tortured. The mage's face lost all color, and she collapsed back to the ground.

"Hold her shoulders and legs down," Perric said. He returned to his prayers and the glow pulsed a violent, dark red that almost bordered on black.

Lithia grabbed Jileli's legs and Saria moved to do what the paladin asked. The slight frame of the mage shook, but she stayed flat.

"It's not working," Perric said with a gasp. Sweat dripped off his face and down his arms. Saria had seen the big man run in full armor and not break a sweat.

"Keep trying or she'll die." Saria shifted one hand to feel for a pulse. It was there, but it was shallow and weak. Saria gripped the mage's face in her hands. "Jileli, fight. Perric is trying to help you."

Blood welled up between Perric's fingers and he continued his healing efforts. The wound appeared to be growing. The paladin removed his hands and sat back in disgust. "I'm sorry. My healing is making it worse."

"You don't quit," Saria growled at him. "There is still a chance."

Tears glistened in his eyes, but he nodded. He gently placed his now bloody hands on either side of the wound. "In Drohara's name, I heal you."

The dark, pulsing glow of his magic resumed. Saria reached down and placed her hands on Perric's, as a sign of confidence. They locked eyes. "You can heal her. By all the gods above and below, you can do this. Remember that half of her is elven and all of her is our teammate."

Perric shook his head, but then his eyes widened in shock. The dark energy flickered from dark to pale and then to a reddish gold...and the wound slowly began to close.

Thank the gods, and Drohara in particular. With her support, Perric managed to force the holy spell past the resistance of Jileli's half-demon side and coax the mage's slight body to heal.

Their fingers interlocked, Perric's prayers sped along like an arrow. After a minute, the wound was but a jagged red scar across the mage's belly.

"How?" Lithia asked. "She was almost dead. Your prayers weren't working."

"I don't know," Perric said, falling away from Jileli, who muttered something unintelligible. "Perhaps Drohara did touch her elven side? It truly was a miracle."

"Could you keep it down over there, I'm trying to die in peace," Ayre said from where he sat, head cradled in his hands.

Saria flopped on the ground next to Jileli. The coloring in the mage's cheeks had returned and her breathing was normal. They'd need to get a fire going and forage for game if possible. Meat would strengthen the mage far more than travel rations.

Lithia sat next to Perric. The archer had a gash along her forehead where the gnoll had struck her. Perric knelt next to her and placed his hands on either side of her head. In seconds, the wound healed, leaving only the faintest trace she'd been injured.

"Thank you," Lithia said softly.

"We'll need to feed her," Perric said, reading Saria's mind. "She'll need meat to recover the blood she lost."

Lithia pushed herself to her feet. She tracked down her bow from where it landed in the wet grass. "I saw a couple of hoof prints. Let me see what I can do."

"Be careful," Saria said. "There could be worse things in the trees."

Lithia laughed. "Let them try to find me in the dark forest." She turned and jogged into the woods, vanishing without a noise.

Saria stood and searched for her fallen weapons. Her dagger was sticking out of the huge gnoll's head. It took a couple minutes to locate her sword, but it was unscathed. The rain had slackened, but a persistent drizzle continued.

Perric chewed on jerky while he watched Jileli's silent form on the ground. The paladin still looked like he was shocked. "You going to make it?" Saria asked.

"Yeah," Perric said after a long pause. "I could feel the healing flowing through me as I prayed, but something fought me. When your hands touched mine, the resistance fled. I've never heard of anything like that before."

"I only lent you the confidence you needed," Saria guessed. Unlike when he'd healed Olive, Saria hadn't accidentally seen Drohara. She hadn't felt anything but fear that Jileli would die. "And reminded you what to reach for."

Perric didn't look convinced. "I suppose."

"Are you done blathering on?" Ayre asked. "I've got a killer headache and you are making too much noise."

"Welcome to the land of the living." Saria walked over to where Ayre sat on the ground. His hands still held his head. She'd felt like that many mornings after long nights of drinking. "How badly are you injured? I'm not sure Perric is up to healing anyone else."

"I just need a beer or ten and I'll be fine," He raised his head and noticed Jileli laying on the ground. "Is she…"

"Dead? No, Perric healed her. We need to make camp for the night. Lithia is hunting," Saria said, filling in the injured thief.

"A shadow fae hunting? They like the elven forests as much as trolls like the sun." He considered for a moment before adding, "She is an odd one, though, so who knows?"

"Aren't we all?" Saria said with a chuckle.

11

Since the rain continued through the night, the Blades erected a makeshift tent and cooked part of the deer Lithia had taken down. Jileli woke during the night and Saria fed her raw venison until she could eat no more. Within minutes, the blood mage was out cold.

"Sleep well," Saria murmured, watching Jileli rest. Losing another one of the Blades was one of her greatest fears. She deeply missed Olive. The ranger had been a safe place for Saria, cool and composed in every situation. Yes, all of the troop understood the risks, had lost friends to the monsters, and been wounded many times. But Saria still felt the keen sense of responsibility to protect them from harm.

Perric stood watch on the other side of the camp. Saria knew she should sleep, but her mind refused to quiet. Thoughts of her encounter with Brar, the fight through the temple, hell, even the stupid bounty they were on warred for her attention. It turned into a stew of half cooked thoughts and raw emotion.

Should they have taken Brar's offer? The gold would have allowed the Blades to retire if they chose, but to where? Even after the Eylnian Empire's collapse and a hundred and fifty years of strife, the monsters were still in charge of most of Southern Holm. The other nations of the world on different continents hadn't fared much better, according to the few sailors she'd met. Tales of impossibly large sea monsters, homicidal mermaids, and undead pirates were told over pints of ale in the local taverns. Were they true? Possibly, but it didn't matter. Saria wasn't setting sail now, or ever, if she had her way. The land was bad enough, but the ocean was a harsh mistress.

"Can't sleep either?" Lithia asked from behind Saria.

She twitched in surprise but settled back. "Worried about Jileli."

"You being exhausted won't help her," the archer said, sitting down near the pitifully small fire. The wet wood smoked and popped while the fire smoldered resentfully at the outside edge of the ramshackle shelter. The smoke swirled around in circles before climbing away from their camp.

"I know." Saria fed a few pieces of somewhat dry wood to the fire. The flames flashed a deep red before returning to normal. "We'll see how she is in the morning. Perric's healing should have fixed the worst of her wounds, but she'll eat like a horse for a few days."

"Healing will do that to you," Lithia said with a low chuckle. She stilled before catching Saria's eye. "I meant to thank you for backing me up with Kranthal. I've been kind of an outcast. It was a situation I've faced far too often, but for once I had a team at my back."

Saria nodded. "We all have secrets, so you don't have to answer, but why did you leave your homeland?"

Lithia stared at her hands. Her long fingers worked at her palms like they were a magic lantern that would give her the answer. Saria wasn't sure what to expect.

"It's not a story I've ever told," Lithia said softly. She still watched her hands, but she continued. "A few years ago, I was married to a warrior in our clan. He was skilled with a sword, but he was also a drunk and a womanizer. The clan elders thought I was strong enough to control him. The elders choose your mates and there are no exceptions made."

The shadow fae's eyes held a haunted expression. Saria watched as Lithia relived the memories of that time, feeling empathy for the other woman. She knew far too well the hold your past had on you.

"The elders were wrong." She pulled a flask from her belt and took a long pull. She handed it to Saria. "Nobody could have been strong enough to control him."

Saria nodded her thanks and took a swallow. She coughed when the bitter liquid hit the back of her throat, before the burn of the alcohol set in. It tasted of brackish water with something dead in it. She handed the flask back.

Lithia took another swallow. "He didn't want to be married and definitely didn't want to give up whoring and gambling, so one night he decided if I was dead he'd have his freedom."

"That seems pretty extreme," Saria observed. Lithia wasn't projecting a lot of emotion, but it was definitely there. "I'm glad he didn't succeed."

"He still ended my life," Lithia said with a shrug. "He attacked me, and I got lucky and stabbed him in the heart when he stumbled. He was so drunk he could barely speak, but he could fight. If he'd been sober, I would be a corpse."

"What happened after?"

"I went to the elders and explained what happened, but they called me a liar and branded me krova or outcast. I was whipped and cast out of the village. The only way I can return is I submit to being a slave, and I refused."

"You've done well for being cast out."

"All children are taught to fight and to use bows in case of attack. I had a natural talent for it, so when a group of the clan's men hunted me down to take me back, to make an example of me. I killed them and took their weapons. After that, I joined up with Butcher's Brigade outside of Auano and hunted smaller monsters."

Saria didn't respond. She'd heard of Butcher's Brigade; they were lower level but and had a reputation for delivering results. The other woman's story wasn't complete, and she didn't want to stop her if she had more to say.

"One night, about six months ago, we were hunting down a pack of goblins for a local farmer. They had butchered half his flock." Lithia took another drink from her flask. "We had tracked them to the river and had decided to camp for the night and continue in the morning. I was standing second watch when an arrow took me in the shoulder. It knocked me into the river. I can't swim well, but I managed to not drown and finally made it to shore. When I backtracked to the camp, they were all dead. It wasn't goblins that killed them. I saved the arrow." She reached into her quiver, pulled two pieces of an arrow out, and handed them over.

Saria took the arrow and studied it in the flickering light from the fire. Blood had dried on the fletching and shaft, but the head was intact. Lithia must have broken it off to remove it from her shoulder.

She smelled the shaft. Cedar. Only professional fletchers used cedar. The goblins used much shorter arrows with barbed headed tips for hunting. "No goblin bow could shoot this. Far too long. This was a professional's arrow."

Lithia's eyes widened slightly. "Correct on both counts. Butcher's Brigade weren't professionals, but they were tough and good in a fight. They were murdered, but I have no idea why or by who."

"Instead of returning to town, I decided to lie low and

recover from my wounds. Once I was able, I began practicing so that I could join another troop."

"The Blades are lucky to have you," Saria said. She handed back the arrow and watched her carefully put it away.

"The only saving grace was it wasn't poisoned, or I'd be dead."

Assassins after another troop six months ago. Saria had to wonder if this was connected to the assassins sent after the Blades and Clan Chaos. Troops sometimes disappeared, and it was always assumed that monsters had done the deed. Or vicious necromancers like Lady Calrur. Nobody would notice if assassins had been decimating the troops, yet it made no sense that they would do that. All the troops were needed to protect the civilians from monsters.

But she didn't say this aloud to Lithia. Instead, she said, "Sorry to sound callous, but skipping the poison was sloppy work."

"I agree," Lithia said before taking another drink. "They were professionals, and we were not. Probably didn't want to cut into their profits by buying poison. Didn't think they needed to."

Saria laughed. "Thank the gods they were cheap."

They both laughed until a noise from Perric stopped them. Lithia handed the flask back to Saria. She wanted to refuse the vile stuff, but since Lithia was offering, she did her the honor of accepting.

The more she drank, the more she wished she hadn't.

12

The sun rose, much to Saria's chagrin. Whatever was in Lithia's flask had knocked her on her ass. She pushed herself out of her tangled bedroll, stumbled to the edge of camp, and loudly threw up.

"Wow," Ayre said as she returned to the camp. "That was a monumental episode of spewing. Too bad we don't have a bard with us. What a ballad it would be. Saria, the projectile vomiter. It would be all the rage in the taverns across the continent."

"Shut up before I skin you alive," Saria growled at the laughing thief. "Lithia tried to kill me."

"It was quality Svartan black ale," Lithia said from where she sat, checking over her arrows. "That flask alone cost quite a few silver pieces."

"I've heard that is nasty stuff." Perric was in the process of breaking down camp. "You probably should have passed."

"Fuck off," Saria snapped. "I'll curse you from the grave."

Ayre tossed her a small vial. "Drink that. It will cure your hangover."

Normally, she'd have questioned Ayre about what it was

exactly, but the way she felt, if it killed her, she'd count it as a blessing.

Jileli sat up slowly. "What happened, and why does my mouth taste like death?"

Ayre went over, checked her where she'd been cut, and told her the story. As Ayre embellished what should have been three sentences, Saria's head started to pound less, more like a stampeding herd than the avalanche from earlier.

Jileli interrupted Ayre when he got to the part about eating venison. "You fed me meat? No wonder the taste is so rancid."

Perric handed her a waterskin and the mage drank greedily from it. "Thank you, Perric. I know it had to be difficult to heal me."

He didn't look at her when he answered. "It was difficult, but you are a Blade and would do the same for me."

"I would, but I'm not sure you'd thank me for it."

"We have different methods, but we are protecting people and keeping each other alive. My personal beliefs don't matter when it comes to the Blades."

Saria almost felt like smiling. That was a big step for Perric. For whatever reason, he still held a dislike for the mage, but he'd pulled through when her life was on the line. "Jileli, can you walk or do you need more rest?"

"As long as we don't push, I can make it."

Saria pushed to her feet, only slightly wobbling in the process. Whatever was in the vial had worked. "Pack up and let's move out. In three days, we should be in Coldbrook."

Three days later, the Blades stood before the steel-banded wooden gate at Coldbrook. Two bored guards lounged in the tower that flanked the gate. "What's your business?" one asked.

Perric stepped forward. "We are on a bounty to find a missing man, and the last place he was seen was here."

"Fine," the guard said. "Jax, open the gate."

The gate creaked open. Once there was room to walk through, a bearded man with wild hair peered around the edge of the door and spoke, his word slurred. "I ain't pushin' this thing all the way fer just the few of you."

Perric nodded to Jax. "Thank you, friend. May Drohara's light illuminate and protect you and yours."

Jax spat in the dirt. "Gods done abandoned us when the monsters came."

Saria put her hand on the big man's shoulder and guided him past the drunkard. "Thank you," she said to the gate-keeper as they went by.

Ayre, Jileli, and Lithia followed. The guard watched them with interest. "I ain't never had me no woman with horns. You want to have some fun?"

Jileli smiled and approached the man, who stood grinning like the fool he was. "I sure do."

"Let's go," he said with a leering smile.

Jileli leaned in and whispered in his ear. All the color fled his face. His mouth dropped open as the mage continued to talk.

"That's disgusting," he said, backing away, making the sign to ward from evil. "You stay away from me."

Jileli stepped closer, reaching for his hand.

He turned and fled. Laughter from the guards followed him like his stench.

"What did you say to him?" Lithia asked with a mixture of shock and amusement on her face.

"I described the mating rituals of a few demon species I've

heard about, but only the very worst ones. I guess he doesn't have the stomach for such things."

Ayre burst out laughing.

"Come on," Saria said, trying, and failing, to keep the humor out of her voice. They had visited Coldbrook any number of times during their missions, and there was one place in town that might have information about a missing man. "We need to check around for our bounty."

Perric led the way to the Rusty Bucket. The tavern had seen better days, as had the town. The unused horse troughs out front had fallen into disrepair. Horses had mostly been attacked and eaten when the monsters arrived. Royalty still had horse farms behind walls with archers to protect their stock, but a hungry giant or griffin would make a meal out of a horse given the opportunity. Cows, sheep, goats, and the like had fared somewhat better, but all had to be protected as vigilantly as the people.

A small bell tinkled when Perric opened the door. The common room was a collection of beat-up plank tables with benches that guaranteed a splinter in the ass for anyone unlucky enough to slide across one. A human woman of middle years, graying hair, and a sour disposition stood behind the bar.

"Lunch is over or are you wantin' rooms?" she demanded as they entered.

How bad would the beds be in a tavern that was this poorly maintained? "Just information."

"Go somewhere else," she said with a sneer plastered across her face. "I got no use for you troopers. Come in here and bust up the place or each other. A bit ago, some trooper started goin' on about hunting wyverns, but they were gonna find a dragon to kill. Bah, they died off a long time ago. When the locals told em so, a fight started and they ended up knocking the crap out of the townsfolk. Constable kicked em out of the city. Serves em right. I run a respectable inn, not a soldier hangout."

"What troop was it?" Saria asked. Had Chaos Clan started that fight? They weren't usually so belligerent, but if they got pushed, they would push back. Hard. It was possible they had come through here while tracking down Lady Calrur, who had been rumored to be in the Ganlam Woods. No, probably a troop like Skull Posse. Or, she should say, the late and not so great Skull Posse.

"Don't know and don't care," the innkeeper responded.

"Madame," Ayre said with a flourishing bow. "If we could trouble you for a moment of your time. Obviously, you are a wise citizen and I can tell you've a keen eye. I'd like to show you a drawing of a man who's gone missing."

A small smile replaced the sneer. She ran her hand through her hair as if straightening it to impress the thief. Saria groaned on the inside, but she couldn't argue that Ayre got results.

"Well, I'm a busy woman…"

Ayre struck his forehead lightly with his palm. "Of course," he said with a bright smile. He fished two silver pieces from his pouch and twirled them on his knuckles. They danced back and forth until they popped into the air, where he snatched them. "I am happy to reimburse you for your time."

Her eyes watched the coins like a hawk. "How could I say no to that? You'll be helping a poor woman with many mouths to feed. Show me the drawing."

Saria retrieved the parchment with the bounty information and the drawing of the missing man. The woman pulled her eyes away from the smiling Ayre and glanced at the paper. Her eyes rolled up into her head and she began to speak in a voice not her own.

"Welcome, travelers," she began, her tones rumbling and

deep. "I was forced to move on from here. I will leave word at the Whiskey Well in Auano as to my whereabouts. People are hunting me, so be wary of who you trust."

The woman's eyes returned to normal. She considered the drawing for a moment before answering. "Might look familiar, but I don't know for sure if I've seen him."

Ayre glanced at Saria, who shrugged. He flipped the two coins back into the air, caught them, then placed them in the tavern owner's hand. He kissed her closed fingers. "Madame, thank you for your hospitality."

"Don't you want a room?" she asked with a big smile. "Dinner isn't for a while yet."

Ayre's face took on a pained look, and he slowly shook his head. "Alas, my companions and I have sworn not to rest until we find this man and return him to his family."

Disappointment shone in her eyes. "Well, you are always welcome here."

Ayre bowed low and then left the tavern. The other followed him out the door. "That was interesting," Ayre said.

Saria started to reply, but a figure crept out of an alley across from the Rusty Bucket. She realized she knew the half-elf woman. It was Belrion Endi, thief of the Chaos Clan. The woman wore more dirt than clothes, which didn't bode well for the rest of the troop.

Saria raised her voice. "Belrion, I need to speak with you."

The woman's eyes flew open in terror. She turned and bolted down the alley.

"We've got to catch her," Saria shouted as she pursued the thief.

The chase was on.

13

S aria flew across the hard-packed dirt road that led through the center of Coldbrook. Her legs pumped, propelling her after Belrion. The woman might know where Talos was. She owed it to Regina to find her son, or at the very least, to find out if he still lived.

"Belrion, we just need to talk," Saria shouted as she chased the nimble thief.

After glancing over her shoulder, the thief increased her pace. Her long blond hair streamed out behind her as she ran. She wore leathers, but they were torn and covered in grime. Saria had seen cleaner pigs.

"I'll head her off," Ayre yelled as he peeled off to the left and raced down the street. Due to his long life, much of it spent as a thief, Ayre knew all the back alleys and secret ways through most of the towns and cities of Southern Holm.

Saria entered the narrow alley, jumping over a stray cat that meandered across the opening. Smells of rotting food, vomit, and decay reached her as she plunged deeper into the space between buildings. The dirt bore stains and puddles from the slop that had been pitched here. The alley took a sharp left.

Saria slowed and peeked around the corner. She spotted Belrion's back as the woman took the next right. Saria charged after her quarry. She didn't know the woman well, but they had shared an ale or two in better days at the troop faire.

A bald man carrying a crate backed out a wooden door and Saria swerved to avoid him with a warning shout. The man jumped back and returned her shout. "Get the hell out of here!"

She raised a finger in response, not wanting to lose Belrion to teach the oaf some manners.

After a series of twists and turns, Saria found herself face to face with Belrion. The woman stood, daggers in both hands, her back to a dead-end wall.

"What the fuck do you want?" Belrion asked. Her tone was hostile, but her eyes flickered around, looking for an escape.

"I just want to talk," Saria said, raising her hands to show her they were empty. "The Mistress of Bounties asked me to find her son, Talos."

"I don't know where he went after…"

"After what?"

The thief spun her knives through her fingers. Ayre did the same when he was nervous or tense. "It's none of your fucking business. Leave me be or I'll make you wish you had."

"Interesting," Ayre's voice came from above them. Saria didn't take her eyes off Belrion, but the half-elf's gaze flickered up.

Ayre sat on the edge of the roof to Saria's left. He had a dagger out, cleaning his nails as if he didn't have a care in the world. "I don't think that is a very polite way to answer the leader of the Shadow Blades, or another trooper for that matter. Maybe being in Chaos Clan has affected your hearing."

"I hear just fine."

"Belrion, I just want to know what happened to you and your band. Last time I saw you, you were decked out in new leathers and wielding silver daggers. Now I find you looking like a beggar and threatening me with eating utensils. What happened?" She kept her voice calm and friendly, but there was a core of iron to her words.

"Just leave me alone," the thief said, her tone pleading, on the verge of begging.

"Tell me what you know, and we'll part ways as friends," Saria said. Should she bring up Lady Calrur in the open or wait?

"You know how humans are," Ayre said with a chuckle. "Short lived, so they are always in a rush. You might as well answer her. She's not going away."

Belrion's shoulders slumped, and the knives lowered. She glared at Saria before answering. "Fine."

Ayre stood and dropped off the ledge to the ground next to Saria. He grasped his nose to shut off the odor. "Gah. You would think they would throw their waste over the wall, not between the buildings. Let's have a drink while we talk."

"You paying?" Belrion asked.

Ayre jerked his head toward Saria. "She is. Looks like you could use a meal as well."

The other's eyes lit up at the mention of food. "I could eat."

"Follow me." Ayre strode down the alley like he was the grand marshal of the empire's military parade. He backtracked a couple of turns and then pounded on a wooden door. A sour old woman threw it open, glaring at Ayre. "Customers enter through the front."

Ayre bowed low. "Madame, I hear the breaded lizard tastes like chicken."

Her eyes narrowed, and she studied his face. "The naga steak is better."

"Ah, but my friend and I crave lizard and a tankard of ale."

The woman stuck her head out and checked both ways. She held out her hand. "Let's see your coin."

Ayre pulled out his coin sack and handed the woman a burnished steel token, but it wasn't a coin like Saria had ever seen. She checked both sides before returning it. "Down the stairs you go, brother."

"Mistress, thank you for your hospitality."

"Just make sure they keep their mouths shut about this place." The woman turned and retreated into the building.

Ayre gestured for Belrion and Saria to follow him in. They descended a narrow set of stairs to a stone walled basement. Three tables sat in the flickering light of table lanterns. Each table held four mismatched chairs of questionable strength. A damp, musty odor filled the room. Ayre took a seat at the table farthest from the door with his back to the wall. Saria indicated for Belrion to have a seat and then did the same.

"What is this place?" Saria asked.

"Safehouse for the Brotherhood of the Silent Knife is my guess," Belrion said. "I hadn't heard about this one."

Ayre nodded but didn't say anything. A moment later, a young woman with pale skin and light hair carried in three tankards and a plate of meat, cheese, and bread. She wore a homespun smock with a stained apron over it.

Belrion started eating as soon as the food was on the table. She shoved a piece of meat in whole and chomped on it like she hadn't eaten in a week. Maybe she hadn't.

Ayre flipped the server a silver coin, which she caught out of the air. The woman left without a second glance.

Saria waited for the carnage to slow before saying, "So, out with it. What happened?"

Belrion swallowed her food. "Well, it all started at the troop faire."

14

"We had just come back from a bounty outside of Cloni," Belrion said, wiping her mouth on her filthy sleeve.

Saria wasn't sure if it cleaned her face or made it dirtier. In the enclosed space, she could tell the thief had gone without a bath for a rather long time. She had difficulty wrapping her mind around the fact that the wretch huddled over her meat and cheese was the immaculately dressed Belrion she'd seen so many times at the troop faires.

"After a few days of spending some of the gold we'd earned, we paid the vig on a new bounty. One that was closer that Cloni, though that one had been worth it." She drained her mug and stared mournfully into the empty glass.

Saria pushed her untouched ale to the half-elf. After Lithia's strange concoction, alcohol didn't sound overly appealing.

"Thanks," she said, before taking a big slurp. "I suppose you heard we took the bounty on Lady Calrur?"

"That is the word on the street," Saria said carefully. "Was that the mission you were on when things went sour?"

"Yeah, we should never have taken that bounty. Talos might be a master of eldritch magics, but going after a necromancer?" Belrion shuddered. "But Karfer was always wanting to conquer bigger and bigger foes. It wasn't even about the gold. It was the glory. He was obsessed about taking down a dragon. Said it would make us legends. He settled for a necromancer on this bounty."

"There hasn't been a dragon sighting for over fifty years until—"

Saria kicked Ayre under the table before he divulged that they'd seen a dragon on the way here. Under the best circumstances, people would think they'd been in their cups or were liars. The worst outcome would be panicking people. A large number of smaller towns were barely surviving. It'd been over one hundred twenty years since the Eylnian Empire had collapsed, destroying trade and any sense of safety.

Belrion shook her head, her gaze fixed on the mug. "A dragon would have been easier than what we encountered."

If she'd noticed Ayre's gaffe, she didn't show it. Of course, at the rate she downed her ale, Saria doubted she'd be noticing much at all in a short while.

"Before you left to hunt Lady Calrur, did you happen to get in any fights with Skull Posse?" Saria asked next, not mentioning the death marker.

"No?" Belrion raised an eyebrow that had what looked like a fresh scar through it. "Why?"

She shrugged. That was as she'd expected. Skull Posse wouldn't have survived an attack on Chaos Clan. "Their rank increased, and they've been fighting with a lot of troops lately."

"Are you going to let me finish?" When Saria nodded, Belrion continued. "We took the Calrur bounty. We packed up the next day and headed out, through the Ganlam Woods

75

near Misty Top Range. Karfer saw a wyvern, so we spent over a month trying to track it down. Like I said—obsessed. When we returned to the bounty, there was no sign of Calrur, so we skirted the Misty Top range for a time. We reached the Eternal Groves and decided to go in. The elves have no love for necromancers, either."

"That's a long trek," Saria said. A journey that far could partly explain why Chaos Clan hadn't been seen in such a long time.

"It is. We discussed turning back, but Karfer wanted to take down the necromancer." She stared at the table for a few moments before she continued. "We'd been in the Groves for a couple of days when we started noticing strange things."

Ayre's eyebrows quirked. "What kind of strange things?"

She took another hard pull from the mug. "Things like piles of skulls or people crucified on the side of ancient trees. Creepy shit like that."

"That's to be expected around a necromancer," Ayre said, exchanging a glance with Saria. Necromancers were very rare, but the undead they raised continued to be a problem until they were chopped into small enough bits to quit attacking people. It certainly wasn't a job the Blades would have been willing to take, but from the sound of this Lady Calrur, something did need to be done about her.

Belrion closed her eyes. "If only we'd heeded the warnings."

At the haunted expression on Belrion's face, Saria's palms went clammy, and a chill ran down her spine like the icy touch of death. She didn't like where this story was headed and the consequences it had for Talos's mortality. But if Belrion knew for a fact Talos was dead, surely she'd have led with that.

Belrion composed herself and continued. "After the fourth night, noises were coming from deeper in the forest.

Howls and shrieks would fill the air for minutes, then go silent. This happened over and over until I thought it would drive me mad."

"Did you find out what was making the noise? Some kind of zombie?" Ayre too pushed his untouched tankard over to Belrion.

She downed the last of Saria's ale before grabbing the proffered mug. She took a swig. "Where was I?"

Saria and Ayre exchanged a glance. "The noises?" Saria said slowly.

Belrion nodded. "Thanks. The noises kept getting louder, but no matter how we hunted it, none of us couldn't find the source."

"Strange," Saria said, turning the story over in her head. None of this was telling her what happened to Talos, though. "What happened next?"

"After days of trekking through the forests in a grid pattern, we were pretty deep in the Eternal Groves at the southern edge of Mount Penance. We made camp and set our watch. When I woke, I was staked to the ground with the rest of the troop in what I thought was an orc encampment."

"Orcs don't usually stray from the Malachite Desert," Ayre said in a thoughtful tone.

"More importantly, how did orcs capture an elite troop?" Saria asked. "There must have been powerful magic at play, because Talos is one of the strongest mages I've ever met."

"I agree. My guess is they used magic to subdue us, but it is just a guess." Belrion turned the mug around in circles on the table. "Calrur's camp was a mix of all races and monsters, not orcs. The first day she gave Karfer his sword and made him fight an abomination. It had long tentacles and a mouth full of razor teeth. The fight was over in the blink of an eye, but the thing feasted on him while he was still alive. She laughed as the thing ate his guts. Karfer screamed for over a day before he finally died."

Ayre's face blanched. "Karfer was an amazing warrior."

"Not anymore," Belrion said with a harsh laugh. "Then it was my turn. Calrur instructed her goons to take me into a tent. I tried to resist, but I'd been drugged to the point I could barely stand, let alone fight. They tied me to a rack and tortured me for days. Maybe weeks. Nightmare creatures fed on me while the guards questioned me. I thought I would die, but I didn't."

Saria's mouth dropped open, stunned. "What did they want?"

"The bounty had been a trap the whole time to lure us to their camp. They wanted to know information about our last bounty and who we'd talked to. Then they started questioning me about something called Dreambinder. I'd never heard of it, but they insisted we'd discovered it during one of our bounties."

Ayre frowned. "Dreambinder? Why does that name sound familiar?"

Belrion continued. "I don't even know what it is. A weapon? An artifact? A person? I don't know how long they had me there, but eventually, they dumped me in the forest."

How long had Belrion survived such torture? Regina had told Saria Chaos Clan hadn't been heard from in months. "They let you live?" Saria asked.

"Not intentionally." Belrion's eyes were glassy. She stared at the mug like it was a crystal ball. She rocked back and forth as if trying to glean the information she was missing. "They sliced my belly open and left me for the beasts to finish off, but they didn't do a very good job of it. I staggered through the forest and eventually ended up here."

If Saria had her rough geography right, that would have been a trek of nearly five days at a good pace. How had the half elf managed it? "Why didn't you return to Moonbourne and summon the troops? We could have banded together and rescued your team."

She shuddered. "I'd have to go back there." Tears fell down the thief's face, leaving a clean trail through the grime. "I won't return there. I can't face the place after the torture they inflicted on me."

"What do you mean?" Ayre asked gently. "The troops will protect you."

Belrion slammed the mug on the table. "No one can protect me from the horrors I saw there. I've fought all sorts of monsters, undead, behemoths, but nothing like what happened there. They infest my dreams. I wake screaming every time I close my eyes."

"What of the rest?" Saria asked but feared the answer. "What happened to Talos?"

She shook her head. "I don't know, but I hope to all the gods he died before he had to suffer like this. Lady Calrur is a monster. She's using her magic to control her troops like puppets."

"We can take you back to Moonbourne," Saria offered. That would be the quickest way to get this information to Regina.

The woman's face twisted into that of a fearful child. "No. I'm returning to the elven city of Inaris to stay with my family. The elves might be able to hide from what's coming, but I don't know if even their magic is strong enough to save us. Lady Calrur is more powerful than we thought. I don't know what happened to the others, but I hope they are dead."

"It can't be that bad," Ayre said.

"You don't know. When the guards thought I was unconscious, they were talking about Calrur opening a portal to the underworld. She thinks she can use the demons to destroy the Nightmare Queen."

Talk about falling from the frying pan into the fire. Apparently, the Nightmare Queen was still alive and had not one but two vicious magic users trying to do her in. Brar had claimed the same motivation as Calrur. Granted, Brar said she wanted to stop the Nightmare Queen to save the people who lived here, and it sounded as if Calrur wanted to replace the Nightmare Queen directly.

Imagine Brar Opalback being the better option for anything. That was only if you believed her story to be true.

Saria pulled a few coins from her purse and slid them across to Belrion. "That should at least get you a bath and clean clothes. There are traders headed in the direction of Inaris if you wait here. You'll be safer that way."

Belrion sobbed as she clutched the coins. "Thank you."

Saria stood. "May the gods watch over you and grant you peace."

"The only peace I'll ever have is in the grave."

15

Saria and Ayre found the others sitting outside the Rusty Bucket. Perric rose, wiping the dust off his armor. Jileli still looked pale, but nowhere near as bad as just after her wound. Lithia sharpened one of her daggers.

"Did you catch her?" Perric asked as the duo approached.

"No thanks to you, we did," Ayre said with a smirk.

"If you think I can run down a thief in scale mail, you've spent too much time in the sun, my pointy-eared friend."

Ayre laughed. "I don't think you could catch a tortoise in that getup, but it does keep you alive, so it has its uses."

"We need to talk." Saria kept her voice low in case anyone approached. Other than a few carts going by and the occasional outburst of children at play, the streets were fairly empty. "We spoke with Belrion. I'll spare you the details, but Chaos Clan was set up."

The snick, snick of Lithia honing her dagger filled the air. "Set up how?" Lithia asked.

"The bounty they took was for Lady Calrur, but she had a

whole army. They were captured and tortured. Karfer is dead, but the rest may still be prisoners."

"Or undead," Perric said grimly.

Saria took a deep breath. Would it be worse to tell Regina her son was dead or risen from the dead? "We need to go find them."

"If Chaos Clan couldn't best Lady Calrur and this group of monsters, what chance do we have?" Jileli asked. Her coloring was better, but the dark circles around her eyes gave her a frail appearance. Healing demanded a lot of energy, and the small mage was still paying for it.

"We've got surprise on our side." Saria stopped to consider for a moment. "I'm not suggesting we go in and attack the camp. If we can determine whether the other members of Chaos Clan are still alive, then we can rescue them ourselves or get help, depending on the odds."

Ayre scoffed. "Unless there is gold to be had, the other troops won't lift a finger to help." When Saria started to answer, he cut her off. "Look, I know you are close with the Mistress, but in the time it takes to find the camp, get the information we need, and return to Moonbourne, they could all be dead or worse. No, my vote is to follow the lead to find our missing person and then, when we return to Moon-bourne, you can give the Mistress the information she asked for."

"We are five or so days from the camp. By the time we chase down the lead in Auano, if our guy is still there, and return to Moonbourne, Talos and his team will be dead for sure." Saria hated the notes of panic in her voice, but she'd known Talos since he was a baby. The only thing she wanted to do was return him to his mother, safe and sound, or at least bring back his corpse so they could give him a proper burial.

She did not want to have to return zombie Talos to his mother.

Ayre placed his hand on his leader's shoulder. "Talos knew what he was getting into when he joined a troop. And when he went after a necromancer. People die in this business. It's not your fault or responsibility to track him down," Ayre said. His tone was soft but held note of authority.

Saria knocked Ayre's hand from her shoulder. He'd been with her the longest, but her personal code wouldn't let her walk away from this. "The rest of you head on to Auano. I'll catch up."

Perric shook his head. His long, ratty hair swayed behind him. "We are a troop. We swore an oath to stay together."

"I didn't swear any oath," Lithia said. "I'm going with Saria."

"Time to vote," Perric said sternly. "We all go after Talos or stay on the bounty. We live together or die apart. Ayre, your vote?"

"Bounty."

"Jileli?"

The mage looked back and forth between Ayre and Saria. Her brow furrowed and she rubbed her hand across her face with a sigh. "If it were me, I'd be praying to any god that would listen for someone to come save me. I'm going with Saria."

Perric nodded. "As am I." He turned to Ayre. "Will you join us?"

Ayre sniffed. "Just because you are all crazy doesn't mean it won't be an adventure. Let's play hero and go find the lost souls."

"Done." Perric glanced at Jileli before asking Saria, "Do we leave now or in the morning?"

A wan smile creased the mage's face.

The correct answer was to get a restful night's sleep, but

the day was still young enough to make good progress. "We leave now. Ayre and Lithia, can you get the provisions we'll need for the extra week?"

Lithia sheathed her dagger. "Certainly. Anything in particular?"

"Just food," Saria said after a couple of seconds. "And extra medical supplies. Unless you find a Pegasus or a flying carpet."

Ayre laughed. "If we find those, we'll be back much quicker."

The two turned and headed down the street. Perric looked over his shoulder at the Rusty Bucket.

"Go ahead and have a couple while we wait." Saria winked at the big man. "You deserve it after healing Jileli."

"Well," he said with a smile. "If you insist."

"Just remember, it's a long walk," Saria said, returning the smile.

The big man saluted and entered the tavern. Saria took a seat next to Jileli. "How are you holding up?"

"I'm fine," the mage said quickly.

Saria set her hand on Jileli's arm. "I know you haven't been with the Blades long, but you are a full member. Just tell me the truth. If you need the rest, we'll leave in the morning."

"Physically I'm fine." Her eyes looked everywhere but at Saria. "The healing was incredibly hard on me."

Saria frowned. Perric had healed Saria many times over the past few years they'd been taking bounties together. "How so?"

"Gods and demons don't mix well. His healing shouldn't have worked, but somehow it did. At first, the divine power fought with my magic, but suddenly, the energy changed and my body healed. If I'd been stronger, I could have healed myself, but I'd never experienced anything like it."

Perric had said the healing wasn't working, but he was

also surprised when it had. Saria wondered why when they had joined hands the healing had begun to work. Maybe her belief in Perric had helped him overcome the demonic part of Jileli's nature.

"Perhaps it was a test of his faith," Jileli said slowly. "I know very little about holy powers, for obvious reasons."

"Well, you're only half demon and don't exactly live an evil life. I'm truly glad it worked."

She grinned. "Me too. I wanted to discuss it with Perric and hopefully figure out what happened, but he's not overly comfortable with me and what I am."

"Give him time," Saria said, nudging the mage with her elbow. "He's a man and slow as a slug to understand things. If he didn't care about you, he wouldn't have tried."

The first real smile Saria had seen from the mage since she'd been wounded blossomed on her face, to be replaced with a neutral expression. "If you say so. You know him better than I."

Interesting. Strong friendships between all team members were a good thing—and friendships came in many flavors. But first they had to find Talos.

16

Three days later, the Blades were deep in the northern portion of the Eternal Groves with Mount Penance visible in the distance, when they could see between the trees. The sun filtered through the canopy, leaving the forest floor dappled with light and shadows. Birds twittered in the branches above them and smaller animals scurried around as they trudged between the trunks and ground cover. Belrion had shown them the rough location on a map, as best she could remember, and they had been combing this part of the forest systematically.

"Do you smell that?" Jileli said. "There is an odd scent in the air."

"I don't smell anything," Perric said from where he brought up the rear.

"Given your penchant for taverns, I'm not surprised off odors don't bother you," Ayre said.

Lithia, who led the party through the dimly lit forest, halted. "I agree. There is an odd scent, but I can't place it."

"It smells like death." Jileli's tone was thin, a worry line forming between her brows. She turned in a circle as she tested the air. "Something has happened near here."

"Necromancy?" Saria asked sharply. They hadn't seen the piles of skulls Belrion had described or heard strange noises, but since Lady Calrur was part of this, that was even worse than a random monster army.

"Possibly. It isn't clean death or the old magics from the gods below."

"Eldritch magic?" Perric said. Drohara and the other modern gods were antithetical to the elder gods; moreover, the old ways were rare and dangerous. That didn't stop mages from tapping into the never-ending source of magic.

"We must be getting close." Saria's shoulders tightened and her gut roiled with anxiety. What if they couldn't figure out what had happened to Talos? And what if it was all too obvious? "How far away is it?"

Jileli's frown deepened. "We are close. The death is unclean, like demon spawn. It is not anything like my blood magic."

"Keep moving," Saria said, checking the sky through a break in the canopy. The sun stood overhead so it was midday. If the Blades found the camp this early in the day, they'd have time to craft a plan to rescue any survivors. The voice in the back of her head suggested it would also give them time to slaughter those who had taken Talos. If he was dead, she knew she'd kill every last one of them to set the scales right.

Lithia resumed their journey through the forest. The archer's excellent sense of direction meant she had been leading the search for the encampment—and it seemed it had paid off. Jileli and Ayre were behind her, with Saria and Perric bringing up the rear.

"I don't like this," Perric said after a few minutes. "If Lady

Calrur is here, we don't stand a chance given she took down Chaos Clan."

What did they expect? A small army of monsters able to cooperate long enough to conquer one of the strongest troops in the land and ruled over by a necromancer. They had discussed both Brar's prediction of another monster invasion and the shadow fae omens without getting any closer to a theory, for surely if this was a second invasion, the army wouldn't stay near Mount Penance picking off troops one by one.

"Could be," Saria said. After five days of travel, she wanted to break her foes in battle, not tiptoe around ineffectively. She shook her head. Perric had called the vote but sided with Saria when she wanted to rescue Talos. The closer they came to the camp, the more violent and awful her thoughts grew as she contemplated revenge.

"Saria, we need to be careful. If this is necromancy, we must better prepare to fight it," Perric said. The big man studied her for a moment. "Are you listening?"

"Of course, I am," Saria snapped at him. "We won't do anything rash, but I have to try to find Talos. I've known him since he was a baby."

Perric scoffed. "You look young enough to be his sister."

Saria smiled back. "I'm thirty. Save your flattery for the brothels and taverns."

He stiffened. "Now you sound like Ayre."

She sighed. "Perric, you can fuck every wench in the four continents, but you always have my back and that is all that matters to me."

Perric grunted. "Life is short for us humans. I intend to enjoy it."

"As you should."

Lithia dropped to the ground, fist up to signal danger.

The rest of the Blades dropped to the ground. Saria crept up next to the archer. "What do you see?"

"At the tree line," Lithia said, pointing off to the left. "I saw the top of a tent."

"Can you get closer?"

"I can. Hold everyone back. If I don't return in ten minutes, run."

Saria nodded. She signaled the Blades to stay put. "Go."

Like a forest creature, Lithia slipped across the uneven terrain to the brush line of the forest. The archer melted into the shadows and disappeared before Saria's eyes. It amazed her how the shadow fae could blend into the background and vanish.

Ayre crawled over to lie next to Saria. "What do you think?"

"I don't know." Saria studied the area, but nothing seemed out of the ordinary. Belrion had told them to look for skulls and hanging bodies, and they hadn't spotted that yet, but any sighting of an encampment here couldn't be a coincidence. Not to mention the death that Jileli sensed. "I hope that the rest of the Chaos Clan is alive, though I'm not sure what we'll find."

Ayre grimaced. "After talking with Belrion, I don't think we want to find survivors. It might be easier to just kill the poor bastards than deal with them being so broken."

Saria agreed, but her promise to Regina and relationship with Talos drove her more forcefully than the fear of finding the remnants of the troop. Whatever had happened, she was going to find out. She prayed to whichever gods would listen that Talos was still alive.

After five minutes, Lithia walked back to the waiting members of the troop. "I found the camp, but there's no signs of life, and I have no idea what happened."

"By no signs of life, do you mean teeming with undead?" Ayre asked.

Lithia glared at him. "I mean, it's empty."

Saria stood. She pulled her sword from the scabbard.

"I don't think you'll need that, but better safe than sorry." Lithia gestured for them to follow.

Saria caught up with the archer easily. Lithia seemed at ease, not ready for a fight, but Saria wasn't ready to relax just yet. "Can you be more specific about what you found?"

"I could, but I wanted other opinions before I voiced mine," Lithia said as they headed to the tree line.

When they reached the heavy brush that concealed the encampment, Saria pushed through and into the clearing. Eight tents were set in a circle with the remains of a huge bonfire in the center. Nothing moved, other than the flapping of tent openings in the breeze. The smell of decay was so strong that Saria wondered how she hadn't smelled it before. Was that what Jileli and the others had picked up on? Who would have thought necromancy smelled like an unemptied chamber pot after a long summer day?

"Theories on what happened here?" Lithia asked.

It was the blood mage who answered. "I concur with what we feared earlier. I sense necromancy, and something else. I don't know."

"Could it be Lady Calrur?" Saria asked.

"If it were, I would expect to see more signs of it," Jileli said. She sank to the ground. "Something of immense power killed everyone here."

"But there are no bodies," Lithia pointed out. "There should be corpses. Dead or undead."

Saria glanced around, noting the cold firepit, the belongings scattered about. If this camp had been as crowded as Belrion described it and something killed them all, there should be dead bodies everywhere. Had everyone been kidnapped, the same way they had kidnapped Chaos Clan? Had their bodies been dragged away? And the signs of struggle didn't say fight. There were no blood stains in the dirt. They may need to track whoever had left this camp so hastily, leaving all their belongings but no blood and no bodies.

"Spread out and look for anything of use. We need to know what happened here," Saria said, though in her heart of hearts she doubted they'd find anything.

That only lasted until Jileli shouted Saria's name.

17

S aria ran to where the blood mage stood, looking into an open tent. Her call echoed through the silence of the encampment.

"What is it?" Saria pushed the flap of the tent aside with her sword, alert for any threats. She peered into the tent to find a desiccated body in the center of the floor. It was curled into the fetal position as if it was trying to hide from whatever had happened.

Jileli stared at the body. "Is that Talos?"

Saria entered the tent. She flipped the corpse over to see the body was that of a woman of indeterminable age. She wore a leather jerkin and bracers on her forearms. A sword of poor quality laid on the ground under one of the cots to her right. Whatever had killed her had mummified her without leaving any other marks. Saria grasped the shoulders to roll her over, and the corpse decomposed into dust under her touch.

"What kind of evil did this?" Saria asked.

Jileli entered the tent. "If it was only this woman, I'd guess it was a vampire, but the whole of the camp is gone and the scent of necromantic magic is undeniable."

"Where are all the rest?" There might be more bodies in more tents unless any of the people who'd been here escaped.

"They could have fled," Jileli said. "If they were being controlled by Lady Calrur, maybe the spell failed and they all ran."

"Are you sure this is necromancy? Wouldn't there be zombies roaming around?" Zombies did have a particular stench, and Saria didn't smell that, only the peculiar scent of decay.

"Yes, and that part is confusing. If it weren't for the smell, I would say it was the old magics."

"You did say you sensed necromancy and something else," Saria reminded her. This was why a troop always, always needed at least one magic user. Normal people like herself had no defenses and no knowledge of such things. "Could it somehow be both?"

"I don't know. There are more warlocks than magi who use the old ways. The price for that is high, but under duress, there have been times where even the weakest of magic users can access the immense power of the elder gods."

Saria shuddered. In her lifetime, she'd seen monsters without end, foul magics that corrupted the souls and minds of the people wielding them, and now a power so strong it could drain the life out of people that might or might not be necromancy.

Perric arrived. "I've seen nothing alive, but the carrion feeders aren't circling the camp, so there must be no corpses, either."

Saria popped back outside. He was right. The sky held no vultures. Any time there was a battle, various scavengers would wait for the victors to leave so they could feast on the spoils. In fact, not even the normal bird calls and insect noises that should have been present in this area could be heard. The absolute silence that surrounded the camp set Saria's nerves on edge.

Ayre trotted up to the group. "All the tents appear unoccupied, but nothing else looks suspicious. It's obvious people left here in a hurry. Do you want us to search the tents for clues?"

Saria gave him an "are you serious" look. They both knew the thief's fingers were itching to ransack the deserted camp. "Make sure you bring anything of interest to me and all valuables are troop split."

"Of course," the thief said with a wide grin.

Saria shook her head. Here they were standing in an enemy's camp and Ayre acted like it was festival day and he had a purse full of gold to spend. Some days he was just too much to deal with.

Ayre turned on his heel and ran off to the nearest tent. If there was anything of value, he would find it, and perhaps some clues as well.

"What do you want to do?" Perric asked.

The paladin surely wasn't happy to be surrounded by necromancy. It was one of the most evil of magics, next to demonic magic. "Can you and Lithia patrol the border of camp?"

A smile crossed his bearded face. "We don't want any nasty surprises."

Saria agreed.

"I think I'll walk with Lithia," Jileli said.

"Of course," Saria said. The whole camp reeked, and she wasn't sure how the mage felt about it. She wasn't sure how she felt, either. Talos wasn't here, but aside from the one corpse, they hadn't found any evidence of where the people had gone. Did that mean he was alive? Had they escaped? Was there any chance at all that Talos could have done this?

Saria had heard tales of his magical prowess. Belrion had called him a master of eldritch powers, but cleaning out the whole camp would have required him to tap into much more than he normally wielded to take revenge on his captors or to free his troop. Why would it have taken him so long to gain access to his magic? Had he perhaps battled Lady Calrur? The questions far outnumbered the answers. At least she'd followed up on the lead and could tell Regina what she'd found. Perhaps she would know what her son was capable of, and perhaps he would even arrive in Moon-bourne before she and the Blades did.

One thing she did know was that Skull Posse had not assassinated them.

Saria, alternating with Ayre, peered into each tent. It did not appear to be the camp of a wealthy army, messy and chaotic as it was. The main belongings were hammocks or pallets on the ground in each tent and a few small chests plus dishes and sundries. After years with Ayre, she avoided anything with a lock. She'd seen firsthand the needle traps or other ways to deter people from stealing another's belongings.

At last she reached the pavilion on the far side of the encampment. It was a silk tent with red and yellow stripes that stood out like a swollen and sore thumb. She'd seen the like in Whitecrest when the traveling performers came to town. An odd choice for an otherwise basic campground.

She pushed the flap back and looked inside. A large table sat in the center of the room with a few mismatched chairs around it. Ducking into the tent, she approached the table. Runes and other glyphs were drawn in what looked like dried blood. An aura of evil permeated the space.

She ducked back out and ran to find Jileli. The mage walked alongside Lithia, who had her bow out and an arrow nocked. At least she wasn't the only one on edge. "Jileli, I need you to see this."

The mage cast Saria a worried glance. "What is it?"

"I don't know, but you might."

Jileli followed Saria back. She hesitated at the entry to the pavilion. "There is something very wrong here."

"That's why I got you," Saria said. The mage's apprehension at entering the tent was telling. It didn't seem like your everyday average necromancy if it unnerved a half succubus.

Slowly, Jileli inched into the interior to the table. She studied the runes and other drawings, pacing around the circumference and wringing her hands. "This makes no sense. They were trying to summon something from the underworld. It has to be a truly terrible demon because they were bypassing the nexus portals. But necromancy doesn't do that."

"What does that mean?" Saria asked, confused.

"The portals link our world to other dimensions," Jileli began.

It sounded familiar, but… "Dimensions?"

"Other worlds like ours in some way. The monster wars started when the Nightmare Queen opened all the portals at once and summoned the creatures from all the connected worlds. The monsters flooded through to this world where they could kill and feast with few natural predators. No one in our world had fought trolls, gnolls, or any of the other hundreds of creatures that came through. We simply weren't equipped to handle it. That's why the Eylnian Empire collapsed in just a few years after ruling the world for ten centuries."

"And we've been struggling ever since," Saria agreed. She had never heard it explained like that. No wonder everything had gone to shit. It was like introducing a new fish into a pond. It either killed everything or it died.

Ayre pulled open the flap and entered. "Oh, fearless leader. Your presence is requested."

"What is it?" she said, trying to force the irritation from her voice. She wanted to hear more of what Jileli had to say, but if Ayre thought something was important, she couldn't afford to ignore him.

When she and Jileli went outside, he tossed a piece of ivory to her. She snatched it out of the air and cursed when she saw what it was.

It was a Skull Posse badge.

18

S aria stared at it for a moment before reaching into her rucksack and pulling out a small leather pouch. She undid the laces and took out one of the emblems they had found on the Skull Posse when they had fought and killed them in self-defense. Originally the badge was to prove that they'd been attacked, but since Gnedain had never shown up at Moonbourne, they'd remained tucked away in her bag. She held the two out to the group.

"They are the same," Ayre said. "We killed four of the Skull Posse so either Gnedain was here or someone killed him and took his badge."

"We don't know how long it's been here," Saria cautioned. "And people do lose their badges. But this doesn't look good."

"Is it possible that a former member of the Posse was here?" Jileli asked.

"It's possible," Saria said. "Usually, if a member leaves or is killed, they retrieve the badge, but if a member disappeared, they could still have had it."

"Gnedain was a dick, so I doubt he'd allow a former member to keep the badge. The bigger question is why would anyone in Skull Posse be here?" Ayre asked. He spun a dagger absentmindedly through his fingers.

At least a month ago, the Skull Posse had contracted to kill both the Blades and Chaos Clan; that much she knew from retrieving the death markers their attackers had carried. Chaos Clan had been lured here by Lady Calrur or the rumor of her and had been captured, tortured, and questioned about a Dreambinder prior to everyone disappearing. Either Gnedain was working with Calrur or they had caught and done something to him, too. And none of it answered the question of why this group would have contracted the Skull Posse to kill the Blades. Each new piece of information added to the questions.

"What do we do now?" Jileli asked. "I think if I spend more time with the runes, I might be able to divine what these people were trying to do."

"Do that," Saria said before turning to Ayre. "Have you found any traps?"

"No, mostly footlockers or rucksacks. We should go through them just in case."

"Makes sense. Jileli, let us know what you find. Ayre and I will search the tents. I want to be out of here long before sundown."

Both nodded before going their separate ways. Saria studied the scene. She'd known Ayre for a few years, but Jileli was new. She still hadn't quite figured out what she thought of the blood mage. Most troops wouldn't work with one, but Saria was more concerned about having magic to back them up than who was wielding the magic. So far, Jileli was a big asset.

Jileli stepped back into the pavilion. The closing flap broke Saria's pondering. She walked to the nearest tent in the opposite direction Ayre had gone. The flaps were tied back, so Saria ducked into the dimly lit space. The smell of unwashed bodies and cheap alcohol assaulted her nose. Two pallets with thin, ratty mattresses laid on the bare ground with space between them to walk. Motheaten blankets were thrown carelessly on the mattresses. Two leather satchels hung from pegs driven into the tent frame. She took down the first and opened the ties.

She threw the clothes from the satchel on the ground. The owners weren't coming back, and if they did, she'd be long gone. A small pouch contained a few copper coins. A rusty knife in a worn leather scabbard joined the clothes on the ground. She dropped the empty sack.

Well, that was a waste. She did the same for the other bag. There were a few more coins and a half empty flask, but nothing of interest. Whatever had happened to cause everyone here to disappear must have been horrible. Hopefully Jileli could shed some light on it, so she'd have more to tell Regina.

The next three tents yielded about the same as the first. She found two quivers of arrows that appeared to be somewhat good quality. She set those outside the tent for Lithia.

"You found anything?" Ayre called from across the camp.

"Nothing worth much. I've got three more tents to check."

"Four for me, then I'll be done."

"Finish up, then we'll check with Jileli." Saria ducked into the next tent. She rifled through the sacks, leaving the dirty clothes and useless junk on the ground. She turned to leave, but a glimmer caught her eye. Tucked under the mattress was a small wooden box with silver corner guards. It was about six inches on either side and four inches deep. She grabbed a dirty shirt from the floor. Using it as a glove, she carefully slid the box from its hiding place. There wasn't a lock, but this was the type of thing Ayre warned her about. She trotted across the space between the tent rows.

Ayre emerged before she reached the other side as if summoned.

His lips pursed as he spotted the box in her hand. "What kind of interesting trinket did you find?'

She smiled at the thief. "I learned long ago not to open anything, so here you are."

"That definitely isn't ordinary. May I?" Ayre rubbed his fingers together as if to make sure they were ready. He took the box and held it up so the sun reflected off the silver. "Very nice craftsmanship."

"It is a nice box, but what does it hold?"

"Never rush a thief," Ayre said with a grin. His eyes sharpened as he examined the top, bottom, and each side in turn. "Looks clean but stand back just in case."

Saria retreated a few steps.

Ayre rotated the box, so the clasp was away from him, and then he opened it with a flourish. Nothing happened. Ayre whooshed out a big breath.

"What's in it?" Saria stayed where she was until Ayre gave the all clear.

"Wow, it's a ball of metal," Ayre said. The disappointment in his voice was evident. "Why the nice box for a hunk of ore?"

Ayre handed the box back to Saria. "I'm going to go finish searching. At least it's a nice box. Get you a couple of silvers in town."

Saria stared at the matte gray ball that sat on a green silk lining. She touched the metal with one finger. It was cold, colder than the surrounding air. A faint tingle went up her finger as if she'd touched a very warm pot. Not enough to be uncomfortable, but it warned you that it could burn. She gently palmed the ball, testing its weight. Heavier than it looked, maybe a pound, and when her palm got too uncomfortable, she tossed it to the other hand.

She held it at eye level and saw her distorted reflection in it. Her face was dirty, and she looked tired, which she was. She spun it around, but there wasn't a seam or any blemishes. "What do you do, my friend?"

If the ball wanted to answer, it didn't get the chance as unearthly wailing filled the encampment.

19

Saria took off toward the pavilion where she'd last seen Jileli, along with the rest of the Blades. Despite his earlier assurance that he couldn't run in scale armor, Perric reached the tent first. His sword glowed as he threw back the flaps to enter.

"By the holy mother, what is that!" Perric shouted over the unearthly wails.

Saria pushed into the pavilion and stopped dead in her tracks. A ghostly woman floated on the far side of the tent. She was ghastly pale with flowing gauze covering her body. A skeletal hand that ended in talons reached for Jileli. Light flowed from her hand to the center of Jileli's chest. The blood mage hovered above the ground, her back arched in agony.

Without thinking, Saria threw the metal orb at the thing. It flew across the tent, growing as it went. Bands peeled away from it to form a net of metal tendrils. The ball struck the creature and went straight through it. The woman's wails changed to shrieks as if she'd been stabbed.

And she kept shrieking.

Saria slapped her hands over her ears to stop the

ungodly sound, but the keening went on and on, forcing her to her knees. The light suspending Jileli in midair blinked out, and she hit the ground. Perric attempted to trudge forward, but he looked like a man trying to walk into a gale. He strove to reach the creature without success.

"Begone, you foul being. Return to the pit where you belong." He hefted his sword, and it blazed like the sun.

The ghoulish woman's hands came up to shield her eyes. The shrieking continued.

Saria gritted her teeth and forced herself to her feet. Ayre and Lithia were on the ground at the entrance. The wails grew in intensity as Perric's blade shone brighter and brighter until Saria had to remove a hand from her ears to shield her eyes.

All at once the keening stopped.

"Why have you summoned me?" the thing screamed. Wherever the golden rays from the holy blade touched her spirit form, it wavered with ripples. "Why do you bring me forth only to torture me with this vile blade?"

"We did not summon you. Begone, hag," Perric yelled.

"The demon bade me to do her bidding. She spoke the sacred chant. I have upheld my end of the bargain. She promised the soul of an eldritch witch. His touch lingers with the smell of death, but his soul is gone. I demand her as payment."

"You will leave now, or by Drohara's wrath, I will return you in shreds," Perric said. Blood trickled from the big man's ears and nose but he ignored it, though he had to be in agony.

Saria was definitely in pain, with a stabbing inside her ears that seemed to pierce her sinuses. She wiped her face and her hand came away red. Jileli groaned, huddling into herself, so at least she was alive.

Perric advanced on the phantom. He readied his sword to strike.

With a scream of eternal rage and suffering, the ghostly woman fled the pavilion through the wall.

Saria dropped to her knee next to Jileli. The mage sat up, shaking her head. Perric knelt on her other side.

"Are you okay?" Saria asked. Jileli's horns pulsed a gentle purple color like blood pumping through a vein.

"I was stupid," Jileli said, rubbing at her face with her hand. "I was sounding out the symbols and then the phantasm came to me. Whoever is behind this is trying to manipulate a portal spell and instead open a gate into the pit. If that happens, the resulting war would destroy everything."

Saria and Perric stood and helped Jileli up. Perric steadied her as she swayed.

"I'll check on the others." Saria left the tent to see the thief and archer sitting on the ground. Lithia rubbed her forehead while Ayre carefully cleaned the blood from his face with a cloth.

Ayre glanced up. "What was that thing?"

"Jileli called it a phantasm. Perric's blade stopped it from killing her and probably all of us."

The elf gave the doorway of the pavilion a worried glance. "Jileli's had a bad time since she joined the Blades. Once again, some monster has nearly killed her. You think she'll stick around?"

Saria spread her hands. "I hope so. She's good in a fight and can heal."

Lithia shuddered. "Perric told me how she healed the dryad. Gruesome stuff."

"Yet Olive's alive and the orc would have died anyway. I don't much care for how things get done as long as we are all alive at the end of the bounty."

Perric led the slightly stunned Jileli out of the tent. He

paused to toss the metal ball to Saria. "Handy bit of magic there."

"It didn't stop the phantasm," Saria said, staring at the ball like it had let her down. While she wasn't sure what it was, anything that could hurt a phantasm from the pit was a good tool in her book.

"The magic disrupted her presence enough for us to fight it. If she'd fully come into this world, we'd be dead," Jileli said, before she flopped on the ground. "Where did you get it?"

Saria indicated the direction of the living quarters with a tilt of her head. "Tent over there. It was in a box…" She looked around for the abandoned box, spotting it just inside the torn flap of the pavilion. She quickly retrieved it, wiped off the dirt, and stored the ball. She closed it with a click, then placed it carefully into her rucksack.

"That would fetch a good amount of gold." Ayre's eyes lit up. "Now that we know it's a little more impressive than a metal ball."

"It's not for sale," Saria said. Magic items were rare, and a useful one, rarer still. "Might come in handy."

Ayre rubbed his chin thoughtfully. "True enough, but we could probably buy titles with that much gold."

"Titles to what?" Lithia asked with a harsh laugh. "Most of the world is ruled by monsters and the cities that are left are barely holding on. Even with the troops killing monsters for coin, we haven't turned the tide."

"And we won't until the portals are closed," Jileli said. "We should get out of here. I'll tell you what I found while we travel, but I don't want to be here if that phantasm returns."

"Good point," Saria said. "Let's return to Coldbrook. We can pick up the trail of our mystery bounty when we get back."

"What about Talos?" Ayre asked.

Saria considered the phantasm's words about the soul of an eldritch witch. Eldritch magic was quite rare, and Talos's presence here might not be a coincidence. "Nothing we can do for him here. He's either dead or found a way to free himself with his magic, but either way, we can't help him now."

"Do you think that thing was referring to him?" Perric asked. "She said the eldritch witch was gone. Is it possible he was working with these people and it went wrong?"

"He wouldn't be working with them." Saria had known him since he was a kid and, though powerful, he tended to do what was right. The fact that he was on the assassination amulet made no sense if he was part of the attempt to open the portal. "The monster expected a sacrifice, and if that was Talos, I can't imagine he'd hand over his soul to open the pit."

"And I am grateful you all prevented me from taking the place of the missing sacrifice," Jileli said, pushing to her feet. "But we didn't kill it. It simply returned to its realm. Without the doorway open it can't return."

"You closed the door?" Ayre asked.

"I never leave doors open to places I don't know," Jileli said with a grin.

Saria helped her the rest of the way up. "Let's go. I want this place far from us when the sun sets. Lithia, take the lead."

The archer stood, adjusted her bow, and led the troop away from the cursed camp, stopping only to retrieve the arrows Saria had found.

What other horrors they would endure during this bounty?

20

Five days later, the smell of smoke greeted them as they emerged from the forest. Before them, Coldbrook lay in ruins. The walls were scorched and bodies were scattered around the stone walls. Saria wasn't sure if they had died on the walls and fallen off or if the townspeople had thrown the dead outside the walls to be buried later.

But the strangest part was that the charred streaks appeared to be on the outside of the walls.

"What the hell happened here?" Perric said as he stood surveying the damage.

Carrion birds perched on the walls like spots of plague. Part of the wall appeared to have been destroyed by fire. The guard tower where the troop had entered not long ago was nothing but rubble. The heavy wooden door was half off the hinges. It tilted at a crazy angle, like it couldn't decide whether to fall or not.

"It doesn't look very hospitable. Should we go around to the north through the forest?" Lithia asked Saria. "We can pick up the road to Auano on the western side of the town."

"I think we should find out what happened. What if the people from that camp attacked Coldbrook? The fire could be magic in nature."

"Are you sure that's the best plan?" Ayre asked. "We don't know who is in control of the town."

"Good point," Saria said.

"We should definitely go around," Jileli said. The mage looked far improved after a few days of no one trying to kill her.

While Ayre was probably right, Saria had spent her life protecting the people of Southern Holm. If there was anything they could do to help, she at least wanted to offer. And if hostiles held the town, they'd just have to deal with it. "I'm going in."

The four Blades all raised their voices in protest but stopped when she held up her hands. "Look, we need to know what happened. If something is amiss, I can get out and meet you on the far side of the town."

Ayre shook his head. "Wait until dark, and I'll go. I am much better at sneaking in and out. I can discover what happened and report back."

He had a point, but Saria's intuition told her they needed to be away from here as fast as possible. Was it simply a coincidence that the town had been demolished after the Blades had come here on their bounty, or was she beginning to see secret plots everywhere? The off-ness of the situation had her on edge, not to mention someone out there who wanted the Blades assassinated. She wished she could rule Brar out, but the sorceress had been very angry with her.

"Waiting for dark takes too long," she decided. "Lithia, lead the Blades through the forest and find a spot where you can see the road to Auano. I'm going in, asking a few questions, and getting out as fast as possible."

"And if something goes wrong?" Perric asked.

"Then continue with the bounty. We still need to find Elladon Kane."

"I don't like this," Perric said plainly.

He'd become Saria's friend over the years, and she appreciated his loyalty, but you couldn't just stumble across a town that had been razed without checking for survivors, or at least for clues. "Get going. I'll be on the west road in a couple of hours."

"Stay safe," Lithia said before returning to the forest.

Perric clasped arms with his leader. Jileli hugged Saria, fear written all over her face. Saria couldn't blame her after the few weeks they'd been through. Ayre stood rooted in place.

"I can go with you. That way you'd have backup."

"No, the innkeeper made it clear they didn't like troopers, and if we stroll in together it will make it worse. I can go in, find out what happened, and meet up with you on the far side of the city."

Ayre frowned. "I hadn't considered that. I'll kill every last one of them if anything happens to you."

"Appreciate the thought, but I'll be fine." She wished she was as confident as she sounded.

The thief gripped her shoulder and soundlessly vanished into the forest.

She strode out of the shade of the trees and crossed the open fields that the town maintained so they could keep the monsters at bay. About halfway to town, the smell intensified. A mixture of sulfur and decay hung in the air like mist on a rainy day.

She reached the road and set a pace short of a run, but fast enough to get her inside the walls within minutes. Was it rash to enter a town in this condition? What if monsters held the town? Gnolls, giants, trolls or the like could band together for short periods to sack a village, but those tribal types fought amongst themselves as much as they hunted people. She also wasn't convinced they would have used fire to do it.

There wasn't a guard at the gate, which didn't bode well. Peering around the tilted wooden door, she spotted towns-folk walking around the streets. People, not monsters, clad in standard town attire. Carts filled with debris or bodies were lined up along the main road.

After a few minutes of watching, she straightened and entered the town. Buildings were burnt to the ground in some places and untouched in others. Adults were moving rubble from the street or shoring up structures that had lost the building it had been attached to, while children ran errands or tended to smaller children safely out of the way.

She loosened her sword and checked her dagger. She didn't want to fight, but people could be as dangerous as the monsters they hunted. Especially desperate and scared people.

A young boy carrying a pail of water crossed her path. "Excuse me," she started, but the boy's eyes went wide. He dropped the bucket and ran screaming for help. Avoiding the town entirely sounded better and better.

She kept going, keeping her hand off her sword hilt. The last thing she needed was the townsfolk thinking she was there for anything other than to help. She followed the path the Blades had taken the week before and stopped to gawk at the remains of the Rusty Bucket. The building had burnt to the ground. Saria had seen towns set ablaze, but not in such a haphazard way. *What happened here?*

The woman from the Rusty Bucket sat on the steps outside the tavern, speaking with a man holding an ax. He pointed at the husk of the building and gestured. She nodded absently as he jabbered. Her head came up as Saria approached.

111

"You're one of them bounty hunters came in before, ain't ya?" she accused Saria, who stopped in her tracks.

"Yes, ma'am," Saria said, keeping her voice neutral and a smile on her face. "I'm glad to see you, but wondered what happened here."

"I'll tell ya what happened," she said hotly. "A dragon the size of a mountain flew in here and torched the place. Killed a bunch of us. The constable and her men ran it off, but it destroyed everything it touched."

"A dragon?" Saria asked, her stomach hollowing out. The same one they had spotted or yet another one? Either answer boded ill for the Blades. "There hasn't been a dragon sighted in over a hundred years."

"Well, ask anyone. It was a dragon. Where was all you fancy hunters? Nowhere to be found. If there ain't gold in it, you vanish like the wind."

Her companion hefted the ax into a fighting position. "Your kind ain't welcome here. You should go 'fore the constable shows up. You mercs have already caused enough trouble."

Saria scanned the area, seeing an angry crowd of people gathering around her. They were still far enough back, but they listened intently.

"What do we have here?" a loud female voice said from the far side of the crowd. The people moved aside to allow a woman with skin as dark as onyx to pass. Behind her three men, including Jax the gatekeeper, strolled up to stand before her. "What brings you to Coldbrook?"

"She's one of the troopers," the tavern owner said. "Her and her band were in the Bucket 'fore the dragon attack."

"Is that so?" the woman said with a slight nod. "And what bounty were you on? Perhaps trying to kill a dragon? Maybe you lost the rest of your party and here you are. How much gold did you sell us out for?"

Saria held up her hands. "I'm just passing through. We are looking for a man named Elladon Kane. My team went on to Moonbourne to find him, but I wanted to discover what had happened here and offer any assistance I could."

"She's lyin', Anijah," Jax shouted. The bootlicker cowered behind the dark-skinned woman. "They came through the gate all high and mighty. Up to something, I'm tellin ya."

"Well, isn't that interesting," Anijah said. She eyed Saria up like a butcher sizing up a prized steer. "I'm thinking you should spend some time in our jail, just to protect you, of course. I'd hate to see you get hurt."

Saria settled her hand on her sword. Anijah's eyes widened. She might be the constable in Coldbrook, but Saria was a warrior trained and blooded in battle. "Let me leave, and there won't be any more bloodshed."

Anijah's hand went to her sword. "I used to run with Primal Watch. You don't scare me."

"I'm leaving one way or the other," Saria said, her voice as calm as death.

The constable half-drew her sword. This had gotten out of hand far faster than Saria expected and for a far more senseless reason—scared townsfolk looking for someone to blame.

21

Saria stepped back, not wanting a fight. The townspeople were terrified and angry, and she'd walked right into the middle of it. Ayre would never let her hear the end of it. "Look, I came into town to see if I could help, not to cause any trouble. I'll leave and won't return, though I would like to give the town some coin to help rebuild."

Anijah spit on the ground by her feet. Jax and two others moved to flank her. Three more men and women came forward, weapons in hand. None of these were seasoned fighters. Death would come for them if they attacked her. Which was a shame, as these folks needed each other to survive now that their walls had been breached. "We can take your coin and put you to work fixing the damage you caused."

Saria's temper flared. "I didn't have anything to do with what happened here. We were far to the north when the attack happened. I'm sorry for your loss, but I didn't cause it."

"Take her," Anijah said, pulling her sword free from the scabbard.

Saria was a trained warrior. Her reflexes kicked into action. Her sword and dagger were out before any of the townsfolk twitched. An older man with a heavy club stepped toward her. She sliced him across the thigh and kicked him into the two who followed. They went down in a heap.

She pivoted and caught Jax under the chin with her dagger, sending a spray of blood across Anijah's face. The slice was showy, but non-lethal.

"You fools! Come at her all at once," Anijah commanded.

The next two tried to flank her, but she parried the first man's sword, batting it out of his hand. The woman next to him ducked low to get a swing at Saria's legs, but she stepped into the path of Saria's blade. The woman went down, holding her wounded arm.

Saria moved like the wind. The disarmed man thought to run, but he didn't take a step before her blade sliced deep into the backs of his legs, dropping him. He screamed as he fell.

The first trio regrouped and now ran at her, shouting. Two quick swipes of her blade and they were doubly unarmed, having had their weapons removed with surgical precision.

Perhaps nobody would have to die today.

Saria turned to face Anijah. "How many more have to be harmed before you let me go?"

Anijah's laugh was louder than the screams of the wounded. "I'll send you to the pit for killing my people."

"They might not die if you leave me be and tend to their injuries."

Anijah didn't hesitate. She brought her long sword up and slashed it at an angle. Saria jumped back and let the blade whistle past.

Saria slid in behind the blade and sliced a groove across

the other woman's cheek. "That a warning. You can't beat me, and anyone who keeps trying dies."

The crowd backed away from the fight.

Anijah lunged, stabbing her sword at Saria's face.

Saria blocked the strike with both blades and twisted. Anijah held onto the blade, but just barely. The woman had skill, though she wasn't the killing machine Saria was.

Fear blossomed across Anijah's face. She retreated, trying to lure Saria into making a mistake, but Saria had battled against some of the best warriors in Southern Holm and knew all the tricks.

Saria kept her sword at the ready. She waited for the next move.

Anijah charged.

Saria knocked away the woman's blade, but she hadn't expected such a desperate attack. Anijah tackled her, knocking them both to the ground.

The air whooshed out of Saria's lungs as the full weight of her opponent landed on her.

Anijah's fist smashed into Saria's face once, twice, three times. "I'll fucking kill you with my bare hands."

Saria's vision narrowed. She caught the woman's fist in her hand and squeezed.

Anijah's cries filled the air. Saria heard the bones snap as she kept the pressure on. The woman's head bent forward, and Saria smashed her forehead into Anijah's unprotected face, shattering her nose and sending teeth flying.

With a hard twist to her mangled hand, Saria dislodged the woman and grabbed her by the throat. She increased the pressure, intending to cut off her opponent's air supply so she would surrender. But something beneath her fingers crunched and the woman's throat collapsed.

Blood fountained out of Anijah's mouth, covering the dirt road.

Saria dropped Anijah as if the woman had burned her. What the fuck? She'd been in plenty of brawls but had never killed someone who wasn't a monster before. She knew how to pull her punches when needed. A massive troll or an ogre could easily crush a windpipe with a bare hand, but not Saria. She didn't have the strength.

No, she didn't think she had the strength.

The crowd fled.

Anger rushed through her like the blood that came from Anijah's mouth. Why had the constable persisted? Why had she forced this battle she couldn't win? Saria turned the struggling woman onto her side and went to retrieve her weapons from where they had fallen. She spotted her opponent's sword and grabbed it up. It was a well-made blade, longer than Saria preferred, but the quality was excellent.

Anijah writhed in agony, hands on her ruined windpipe. Saria flipped her over and took her scabbard, then she turned her back on the dying woman and stalked away.

She left through the opposite gate and no one tried to stop her. A heat built of battle adrenalin, frustration, and shame propelled her onward and she barely even noticed where she went.

She walked for a short time before she found a shallow stream near the road before it had reached the trees. She washed the dirt and blood from her face, hands, and armor, trying not to relive the feel of Anijah's throat collapsing under her grip. The sound of footfalls warned Saria she wasn't alone.

A lone woman in her early twenties stood twenty feet away. She wore a simple dress of blue with an ornate golden emblem embroidered on her chest, and her long hair was pulled back, showing her elven ears. "I mean you no harm. I just wanted to check to make sure you weren't injured too badly."

"Who are you?" Saria asked. Her voice sounded off, but Anijah's punches had broken her nose. The nasal tone of her voice grated on her nerves.

"I am Nailia, the town healer. The constable was wrong to attack you and I wanted to make up for her poor behavior."

"That is kind of you, though unexpected. I probably don't deserve it." Saria studied the woman for a moment. "How is an elf living in Coldbrook?" While elves were nowhere near as rare as shadow fae, they didn't tend to live in places as small as Coldbrook.

"I was orphaned as a child, and the town healer took me in. Now, I'm a disciple of Era'tal. I returned from the temple when it was overrun and have been here ever since."

She was older than twenty if she'd been trained at the temple of Era'tal. The monsters destroyed all the temples in the first few years of the war.

"What do you want?" Saria said, taking a drink from the river. The water was cold and clean, which helped.

"May I look at your wounds?" Nailia asked. "I promise I mean you no harm."

"Only if you will tell me what happened to Coldbrook. I wasn't expecting that sort of welcome. I only wanted information and was willing to help."

"Deal." Nailia said. She walked over slowly, like she was approaching a dangerous animal. After the fight in Coldbrook, Saria couldn't blame her. The woman knelt by Saria and ran her long, thin fingers over her bruised and swollen face. She closed her eyes and invoked her god.

Warmth flooded through Saria's body. Her muscles and bones moved as the healing mended her. Saria fell forward to lean against the woman.

"Saria!" Lithia's voice came from down the road. "Get away from her or I'll stick you like a pincushion."

Saria tried to speak, but the healer set her hand on her shoulder as if asking her to wait.

Lithia came into view, arrow nocked and ready. "Last warning."

22

"Lithia, put down the bow, she's a healer." Ayre's voice came from behind Lithia. The Blades must have been sheltered in the trees close to the road, waiting for her to emerge. "Can't you see the emblem of Era'tal?"

Lithia lowered the bow and bowed to Nailia. "I'm sorry, priestess. I did not see the badge of your calling."

Nailia's released Saria's head and nodded to the archer. "I would expect you to be a bit jumpy with everything that has occurred."

"What happened?" Ayre asked, concern etched on his features. "Obviously, we should have ALL gone the forest route."

Perric and Jileli arrived on the heels of Ayre.

The paladin bowed low to Nailia. "My lady. What brings a priestess of Era'tal to our aid?"

She tipped her head in a way of greeting. "Holy knight, it is my calling to heal any who require it. Era'tal's temple may be in ruins, but my vows to the holy mother remain."

"As do mine. I am Perric." The paladin gestured to Jileli. "This is my companion Jileli. Lithia is the one with the bow and Ayre is our elven friend. You've made the acquaintance of Saria, our leader."

Nailia's eyes went wide when Perric introduced Jileli, but if she had any comments, she held her tongue. "Greetings. Saria had requested to know what happened in Coldbrook. I followed her after she, um…"

"Defended myself?" Saria offered.

"Yes. The constable and her thugs attacked her for no other reason than she was a stranger. Thanks to Saria, other than the constable, who started the fight, the rest weren't fatally wounded and will recover. If you would sit, I can tell of the attack on Coldbrook."

The Blades all took seats on the ground. Jileli sat a bit back from the group. While the priestess of Era'tal hadn't said anything, certain sects hunted demons and others that didn't fit their standards of purity.

"Thank you for healing me, Nailia, but after I was set upon in Coldbrook, I'm surprised you would risk the wrath of your neighbors," Saria said.

"I heal any and all who come to me in need," the priestess said. "There isn't a person in that town that I've not helped to heal or was there during their times of loss. No one will raise a hand against me."

"That is good," Saria said.

"Two weeks ago, travelers arrived from Moonbourne, telling wild tales in the tavern that they had seen a dragon circling the lands around their city. The locals laughed them off as far-fetched, since dragons were thought to be extinct."

The Blades managed to maintain blank expressions, though it was noteworthy that folks in town had seen a dragon. How could they carefully find out if it the same one that had appeared after they spent several days in the shadow fae's safe house?

"I've not seen signs of one since I was a boy," Ayre said.

"Nor I," Lithia said, lying as smoothly as Ayre. "My father told tales of when the skies above the Malachite Desert were filled with dragons during mating season."

Momentarily distracted, Saria marveled at how old Lithia was. According to the legends, the elder elves could live for a thousand years. Lithia and Ayre and Nailia, for that matter, seemed young on the human scale—younger than Saria, for sure. Ayre had said they didn't choose their true names until they reached one hundred years.

Of course, the elves and equally long-lived dwarves hid from the world instead of fighting to protect it. Perhaps their extended lifespans made them much less willing to risk themselves for others?

"In my youth, I saw many dragons in flight over the Eternal Groves. They are as terrifying as they are magnificent," Nailia said. She paused for a moment. "The stories that the travelers told in the tavern were laughed off, though we were soon to regret our disbelief."

"Interesting," Perric said, exchanging a long look with Saria. They both knew where this was going.

"Four days ago, I heard a huge noise and went outside my house to see what was happening. I thought it to be a storm but was shocked to see a full-fledged red dragon flying above the town. It roared and shook the buildings, but it didn't immediately attack. It appeared to be looking for something."

This time, Ayre caught Saria's eye. Words were unnecessary. The fact that the dragon was red increased the chances it was the same one to nearly a hundred percent, which was both good and bad. Good that there was only one dragon flying around Southern Holm, and bad that the dragon had now been two places that the Blades had also been. Coincidence seemed unlikely in this situation.

"What would a dragon be searching for?" Jileli asked. "Other dragons?"

"I have no idea, but the town folk said that it proceeded to burn the Rusty Bucket to the ground. It left everything else alone at first."

Ayre's eyebrows shot up, but he didn't say anything, for which Saria was eternally grateful.

"The constable rallied the people and attacked the dragon," Nailia said with a shudder. "As you can imagine, it did not go well. The dragon went on a rampage, killing and burning at will."

"Why would it attack a town? I'd understand it if there were large amounts of gold, but, please don't take this wrong, I doubt there are two gold coins in the entire town," Ayre said.

The Blades had been at the Rusty Bucket and received the ensorcelled message from Elladon Kane by proxy. If the dragon had singled out the Rusty Bucket, did that mean it had something to do with Kane? Or the Blades? None of it made any sense. The bounty had been an excuse to get away from Brar Opalback while she cooled off from being turned down.

"No offense taken," Nailia said with a soft smile. "Coldbrook survives on trade, mostly from the bounty hunters who come through and buy food and supplies. Why the constable attacked you puzzles me. You weren't involved in the dragon rampage."

Saria wondered if that was true but kept it to herself. "We stopped in Coldbrook to find a missing person. The tavern owner gave us some information that we left to investigate, only to return to a ruined town."

"The dragon didn't destroy everything. How did the people chase it off?" Lithia asked.

Nailia flushed a soft pink. "I had to protect my people, so I used the power of my goddess to drive it from the town."

"You faced a dragon alone?" Ayre said, his tone one of complete shock. "How are you not dead?"

"I wasn't alone, for the town rallied around to help me, and my goddess protected me. I struck it with a mighty blow of holy force. We were lucky. I thought it would kill us all, but instead it launched itself into the air and fled."

"You drove off a dragon," Perric repeated in awe.

"I cannot say for sure that I did. I don't think it was harmed by my spell, but I thank Era'tal for her protection." The priestess bowed her head for a moment. "Who is the person you seek?"

Saria thought about giving a false name, but the priestess had healed her and told her what she needed to know. It felt wrong to lie about something so inconsequential. "His name is Elladon Kane. His family took out a bounty to find him."

It was Nailia's turn to be shocked. "The Elladon Kane? The wizard? I've heard rumors he's not very trustworthy."

"Most wizards aren't," Ayre said.

Saria's heart dropped. What else could happen on this bounty? She wasn't sure she wanted to know.

23

Y ou know Elladon Kane?" Saria asked. Every time she thought she understood what was going on, something new revealed itself. What had she gotten the Blades into?

"I don't know him personally," Nailia said, holding out her hands, palms up. "He was a high wizard before the monster wars. I'd heard he'd died during the early days of the war defending the dwarven city of Ironhold before the magical defenses were set in place."

"Is he a dwarf?" Ayre asked, a confused expression on his face. "I've not heard the name before."

"No, he is human, but mages live far longer than their mortal counterparts. It wouldn't surprise me if he still lived." Nailia climbed to her feet. "I need to head back to town. When I return, I will speak to the mayor and make sure everyone understands that the constable attacked you unprovoked. I do hope you will stop again under better circumstances."

Saria rose and held out her hand. "If you ever tire of town

life, we could use your skills to protect the people of Southern Holm."

Nailia smiled and shook Saria's hand. "Thank you for the offer, but the life of bounty hunters is one I have no wish to pursue."

"Understood," Saria said with a grin.

"Go in peace, my friends," Nailia said and headed down the road to Coldbrook.

When the priestess was well out of earshot, Ayre spoke up. "How is it that a backwater cleric knows about our target, but none of us do?"

"If he fought for the dwarves, he wouldn't be well known outside of that." Lithia adjusted the fit of her quiver. "I think our friend has a much more interesting past than she's led us to believe."

"I agree," Jileli said. A look of relief came over her face. "Dealing with clerics is stressful for me. Usually, they start screaming abomination and then try to kill me. It was nice to meet a true believer without the judgment."

Saria shook her head. Jileli's life had to be terrible, and it wasn't as if she'd asked to be half succubus. No matter how hard the times were on everyone, there were always people who used their faith as a weapon against others.

Luckily, if you could call it that, Jileli had been born long after the monster wars had begun, and the temples had all been destroyed or abandoned. Not as many clerics running around to try to kill the best magic user the Blades had ever managed to sign on. The rest of the populace had bigger things to worry about than a half succubus mage willing to fight against the same enemy. The ones who threatened her life were limited to a few zealots, or so Saria hoped.

She glanced at Perric, who stood quietly with his arms folded. Did he think Jileli's comment was directed at him? He hadn't wanted to kill her—just hadn't wanted to work with her and had since come around.

"Let's head out to Auano," Saria said before any arguments could start. "At least we have a road to follow."

"For once," Ayre said with a laugh. "One of the few left in Southern Holm."

"Do you think it is wise to be out in the open?" Perric asked. The big man hadn't moved, and the scowl on his face intensified. "Nailia said the dragon went straight to the Rusty Bucket. Does anyone else think that wasn't a coincidence?"

"I had the same thought," Jileli said. Perric's gaze flicked to her but quickly away. "Why a dragon would be hunting us is not clear, but it pays to be safe."

Traveling through the forest instead of on the road would slow them down, but it would be wiser. Of course, if the dragon was looking for them, speed might be their best ally. "I think we stay on the road," Saria decided. "It will be faster, and we can take shelter in Auano and sort things out. It's a much bigger town than Coldbrook and has a standing garrison to help if there is an attack."

"I agree," Lithia said with a shrug. "We need to find out more about where this Elladon Kane is. He must have left a message for us at the Whiskey Well. Do you suppose it will be another ensorcelled innkeeper or will we have to talk to all the stableboys this time?"

Ayre chewed his lip. "I can see both sides, but getting there fast would be the best plan. Plus, we could all use a stiff drink and a warm bed."

"Let's go then," Perric said. He watched the sky for a moment. "Being out here on the road makes me feel vulnerable, but we can be in Auano tomorrow night if we keep up a good pace."

"Five minutes to take care of business and refill water

skins," Saria said. She knelt to filling hers in the cool water of the brook. Perric's shadow crossed over her. She looked up. His face was a tangle of emotions.

"I don't like the blood magic, but you know I'd never harm Jileli, right?"

Saria watched the bubbles flow from the neck of her container. "I do know that. Does she?"

Perric grunted. "I entered Drohara's services well after the temples had collapsed. The local priestess taught us to use our calling as a way to save people, not kill them."

Saria capped her skin, then stood and looked Perric straight in the eye. "We have been friends for many years now. I have never once questioned your integrity. Jileli is new to the Blades, so she had every right to be nervous. If you want her to understand, then speak with her."

"What if she doesn't believe me?"

"Given the tales I've heard you weave for the bar wenches, she might not, but…" Saria paused and smiled at the big man to ensure he knew she was jesting with him. "I think if you aren't trying to bed her, she'll believe you."

Perric's mouth dropped open. "I don't 'weave tales.' I describe our exploits," he said with an affronted tone, but a smile crept in as well.

"So just when did we slay a demigorgon? I distinctly remember hearing you describe that exploit yet have no memory of actually doing it."

"It could have been. It looked like one."

"The farmer whose prize bull you slew in glorious battle might disagree."

"It wasn't a bull," he huffed.

"The meat certainly tasted like beef."

Perric threw his hands in the air. "I can't talk to you when you're like this." His smile beamed.

THE DRAGON'S WRATH BOUNTY

"You mean telling the truth?"

"There's no winning with you," Perric said and stomped off.

Score one for Saria.

24

The walls of Auano rose as the sun set in the west. Saria found herself walking faster though she was exhausted from the forced march to the relative safety of the town. The stone walls were fifteen feet high with a double wooden and steel studded gate in the center of the wall. There hadn't been any sign of a dragon on the trip which Saria was profoundly grateful for.

That didn't mean they hadn't all gotten a crick in the neck from looking worriedly at the sky.

The sun was almost down when they reached the gates. The guard waved them through before the rattle of chains and the shouts from the guards preceded the closure of the town for the night.

Saria approached the closest guard. "Evening, friend. I'm looking for the Whiskey Well. Where might I find it?"

The guard smiled at Saria, though the gnome barely came up to her belt. "Head down two blocks, take a left. Go three more blocks and she'll be on your right."

"Thank you kindly." Saria turned to go.

"I'm off duty in a bit, if you fancy yourself some company while you're here." The guard smiled brightly at her. "I might be short, but I'm stout where it counts, lass."

Saria nodded. "I'm sure you are, but I'll pass for tonight. Leaving early in the morn."

"Can't blame a lad fer tryin'." He gave her a saucy wink.

"Thanks for the directions."

"Well, he was forward," Lithia said as Saria rejoined the group.

"At least he was honest." Perric chuckled.

"I don't know about honest," Jileli said quietly. "I was with a gnome once, and I wouldn't describe it as stout where it counts."

"What?" they all said in unison.

Jileli smiled and shrugged. Her eyes danced with mischief.

"Let's find the Whiskey Well," Saria said, holding back the laugh that threatened to burst out of her. "The sooner we find out our next step, the sooner we can drink."

"Couldn't have said it better myself," Ayre said.

Perric led the way through the streets of Auano. People scurried along, handling the last few errands for the day. Even behind the walls, most people stayed indoors when the sun went down. There were enough monsters that flew to warrant the extra caution.

A cart loaded with someone's belongings sat at the entry to an alley. Had people fled Coldbrook after the attack to take up residence in a new place? Her heart broke for the people of the town. They didn't deserve what had happened.

She also regretted the fight in Coldbrook. The constable and her men had paid the price for attacking her, but they had been scared and lashing out. The possibility that the dragon had partially razed the town on the hunt for them, causing all that death and destruction, weighed on her mind. To have one party who wanted them dead for sure, per the death marker they'd found with Skull Posse, was bad enough, and then they'd pissed off Brar and now...a dragon?

Perric turned onto the street the gnome guard had indicated, and they followed along. The people thinned out as the gas lamps were being lit. The quiet was somehow comforting. Normal people doing normal things. Saria had never longed for that type of life, so her mission was to help people stay safe from the dangerous world that lurked outside the handful of walled towns and cities. The people who did long for that type of life deserved to live it.

After a few more minutes, the sign for the Whiskey Well appeared. The building was painted gray and had stone stairs leading up to a wooden door. The steps were swept, and the place was well maintained. Saria's spirits rose. A clean establishment would have good food, and more importantly, beds without insects.

The troop entered the Whiskey Well. Most of the tables were empty, but a few early birds talked and laughed. The fireplace sat cold, given the warmth of the day. The bar was polished until it almost glowed. A man with a protruding belly covered by an immaculately white apron stood talking to two older patrons. Saria signaled for the troop to get a table and approached the bar. She waited while the barkeep talked with the others.

"Widow Marle told me she'd heard there was a hex on her daughter, but turns out the girl was knocked up by the blacksmith's apprentice." The three men laughed. Saria wasn't sure why it was funny, but they certainly found it to be so. The man behind the bar excused himself and came over to Saria.

"Ho, adventurer. What can I get you this fine evening?" he said in a deep, booming voice. He had a large mustache and thinning hair, but his smile was warm and genuine.

"Five cups of ale and whatever the amazing smell is coming from the kitchen. Do you have something for my elvish friends?"

His smile broadened. "Of course. I have vegetable pies for the meat disinclined, but my cook got a wild boar and made an amazing stew."

Saria's mouth watered. A proper meal was a luxury for troopers. "Two bowls of stew and three of the pies."

His face flushed, and he stammered out, "I hate to be rude, but…"

Saria nodded. "We live in troubled times, friend." She slid two silver coins over and his face brightened. "I'll need rooms as well."

"I've three rooms available. Two beds per. Baths are an extra two coppers per."

Saria slid two more silvers to the man.

"I'll have the rooms readied for ya and your troop. You've covered all the ale you'll be wanting. The Scarlet Rose is just down the street if any are looking fer company."

Saria laughed. "I'm only paying for the rooms and food. They can handle their own entertainment."

He slapped his meaty hand on the bar. "By the gods above, they can. Food will be right out."

Within minutes, mugs of ale and plates of food sat on the table. No one spoke as they downed real food for the first time since Moonbourne. The stew was tangy and rich, thick with potatoes and onions. Saria thought about a second bowl but decided not to risk overdoing it.

"Should we talk to the barkeep?" Lithia asked.

"Let's wait until the place clears out," Ayre said checking the room. "We don't need a lot of ears around if they have the information we need."

Jileli looked over her shoulder. "I've been wondering if the spell Kane is using is attracting… things we don't want to discuss here. Lithia, do you remember anything that could answer that?"

Lithia shrugged and wiped the foam off her upper lip. "Could be, I suppose? But it doesn't answer why now, and why nowhere else that spells are being used."

The Blades sat and drank for the better part of the evening before the last of the locals left for their homes and the other patrons for their beds. There was no reason to endanger the residents if the bounty's magic was attracting the dragon. Saria pulled the parchment out and approached the barkeep. She tossed him another silver in way of thanks. "Thank your cook. The food was outstanding."

"I'll let her know. Anything else I can get ya before I close up for the evening?"

Saria held out the paper. "Does this man look familiar?"

The man's eyes glazed over. "Greetings, traveler," the same voice from Coldbrook said. "Things are worse than they appear. I have retreated to the elven city of Yllle Serinis. Make haste, for you are in danger."

The man's eyes returned to normal, and he looked at the drawing. "Can't say as I do. Friend of yours?"

"His family asked us to find him," Saria said, folding and putting away the paper. "Thank you for your hospitality. We'll be headed up now so you can get some sleep."

"I'll have your baths drawn. The baths are down the hall from your rooms on your left. Helen will have them ready in a few."

"Thank you." Saria returned to the table. "He's relocated to Yllle Serinis."

Ayre's face blanched, but he didn't say anything.

"We head out at first light. Baths are being drawn for all of us. I know this is our first town in a while, but we should stay at the inn, just in case. If anything happens, we'll be here to help protect the inn."

As if she had summoned it, a loud roar filled the air. The tavern shook from the sound. A bright reddish light gleamed on the windows from the outside.

Enough running. It was time to fight.

25

W hat was that?" the barkeep shouted.

Chairs scraped across the cobbled floor as the Blades grabbed their weapons and ran for the door.

"Get everyone out!" Perric yelled at the barkeep.

Saria didn't stay to find out if the man followed Perric's orders. They raced into the street. Screams emanated from all around as the town came to life to face an imminent threat. Guards were running everywhere, yelling orders.

The dragon soared overhead, roaring its challenge. Flames spewed from its mouth and illuminated the surrounding buildings. "We need to find an open area," Perric called from the front.

"The town square," Ayre said, pointing to where they were headed.

Saria pushed her way past a mother fleeing with her baby in her arms. She wanted to take the woman to safety, but if they didn't drive off the dragon—killing it wasn't exactly a possibility—then the whole town would be at risk like Coldbrook.

The town square spread out before them as wagons burned where they'd been left for the night. The oxen that drew them were safely secured inside the pens. A large stone fountain depicting the gods occupied the center of the space. Saria led the team there. "We make our stand here. Lithia, can you shoot that thing?"

"I can get its attention," the archer said. She pulled an arrow and watched.

The massive beast flew overhead, and Lithia went to work. Within seconds, she had put arrows through both wings. The red dragon roared in defiance. Its head swiveled on its serpentine neck until it spotted its tormentor.

It banked into a sharp turn and landed in the square. Saria was amazed at how softly the drake landed. It spit fire at the fountain, scattering the Blades.

"We need to drive it off," Perric said. He lowered his head and intoned a prayer. A golden aura of protection surrounded him as he finished. He charged at the beast, sword held at the ready.

Saria freed her sword and dagger and ran to flank the giant beast. It let out a gout of flame that rolled over Perric, but the paladin shrugged it off and kept going. The aura had faded with the blast of fire.

Arrows whistled through the open air, striking the dragon, but mostly bouncing off. Saria reached the dragon's right wing and hacked at the fibrous membrane. Her sword skidded off without much damage. She stabbed over and over again until the dragon's tail flickered and struck her in the back, sending her sailing through the air.

She hit the ground and rolled.

"Saria!" Jileli yelled over the noise of the battle.

Saria waved her off as she fought to regain her breath. And the use of her limbs, because the dragon bounded toward her where she lay gasping. The creature's mouth widened, as if it would eat her in one bite. She scuttled backward but feared she wouldn't be fast enough.

The shining blade of Perric's sword struck true, taking the dragon on the exposed flesh of its open mouth. The head whipped up in a scream of agony.

A bright blue ray lit the night. Jileli stood, power radiating off her as she threw her magic at the giant. Like all the solid weapons, the magic bounced off the armored hide, leaving it unharmed. But it did give Saria a minute to clamber to her feet and prepare herself to try again.

Ayre darted in low, slicing at the soft spots behind the legs or stabbing between armor plates. The dragon spun, trying to catch him, but the elf was far faster. At this point Saria knew they couldn't kill it, but if they annoyed it enough it might leave like at Coldbrook.

Assuming it wasn't determined to kill them.

Arrows clattered harmlessly into the creature's face. As a team they had unleashed their best attacks and had barely scratched the dragon.

Saria ran and snatched up her sword. Well, the sword formerly known as Anijah's sword. She hefted it, but even this high-quality steel seemed powerless to hurt their foe.

The town guard arrived, armored and toting heavy pikes. They charged in, slamming into the flank of the giant. With a scream of rage, it turned on the new arrivals and shot a stream of fire across them. Some of the troops were fast enough to get behind the kite shields they carried, but others burst into flame. Those unlucky souls were consumed by the fire as the townsfolk ran in every direction.

They were losing. There was no other way to look at it. Even with their combined might, they didn't have the weapons or the magic to penetrate the dragon's natural armor. They needed a plan to chase the dragon out of the town and away from the innocent people who were just trying to live their lives.

What weapon did they have that could slay a dragon? No, she was thinking too big. They only needed to drive off the dragon. While the guards, Perric, and Ayre valiantly engaged the beast, she pulled her rucksack off her back and rummaged through it until she felt the polished wooden box. She yanked it open, dropping the box to shatter on the stone. Meanwhile the dragon chomped down on one of the guards. The woman's screams ended abruptly as the drake tore her in half.

Ball in hand, she waited until the dragon opened its maw to shoot flames. It would be her only chance. The dragon's head struck Perric and sent him rolling across the stones. It lumbered over him, hissing.

Wait.

The dragon reared back, sucking in air for the blast to finish off its enemy.

Saria threw the ball. As it soared through the air, it opened into the same net as before. The sharp metal bands struck the end of the dragon's snout and fastened on like a leech. Fire leaked out the sides of the dragon's secured mouth.

Perric's sword crashed into the dragon's skull. Batting the paladin away, it slammed its head on the ground, looking like a muzzled dog trying to free itself. After a few fruitless tries, the beast's eyes locked on Saria and it advanced. While it couldn't use its mouth, the claws and tail could certainly kill anyone in its way.

"Retreat!" she screamed, then headed for the gate.

If it wanted her, it was going to have to catch her.

S aria and the Blades raced down the street headed for the main entrance. "Open the gate!"

The guards were arrayed in front of the gate, pikes and shields at the ready. "Stand down," the lead guard yelled at the Blades as they ran.

"Open the gate!" Saria screamed, closing the distance between them. She was close enough to see the man's eyes widen as the dragon came pounding down the street behind them.

"Dragon!" he screamed. "Open the gate, now!"

The chains creaked as the Blades ran between guards. Saria turned sideways and slid between the two doors and out into the night. Above her the sound of beating wings alerted her that the dragon was airborne. She pelted toward the forest that lay two hundred yards ahead. The rest were on her heels, though Jileli lagged a bit behind.

She signaled for them to keep running and slowed. When Jileli reached her, she scooped the small mage off her feet and resumed her run toward the trees. The full moon lit the night making it easier to flee and see their pursuer. They reached the halfway point, and the dragon sped toward them, talons out like an eagle snatching a fish out of the water. Saria threw herself flat, careful not to crush Jileli in the process. The intense wind from the dragon passing over them scattered them all with pebbles and sticks.

Perric grabbed Jileli and took off for the trees. Saria said a silent thanks to the big man. Jileli was light but running full speed with her had been taxing.

The dragon swooped in again, aiming for Ayre, but the nimble thief rolled and sliced his dagger across the extended toe, cutting deep. Who knew a red dragon's toes were vulnerable? The dragon lurched back into the sky with a muffled bellow.

They reached the woods and plunged into brush. The dragon landed near the tree line where its prey had vanished. It pushed into the scrub as well, but being the size of a small barn, it was far too large to squeeze between the enormous trees.

Would it attempt to uproot the trees in its pursuit of them? Would it set the forest on fire?

The Blades hid like frightened rabbits while the monster thrashed, trying to get to them, but after what seemed like an eternity, the sound of flapping wings signaled the dragon's departure.

Somehow, they'd escaped the dragon's wrath.

Now if they only knew why—and if—it was hunting them. But it did seem likely at this point.

"Is everyone okay?" Saria asked into the darkness. She could pick out the outlines of her companions, but not their faces. The elves were far better with night vision, and poor Perric was completely blind in the dark. Saria found her light stone and set it before her. It was bright enough to see by, but not enough to attract unwanted attention from outside the forest. If there were monsters in the woods, they would have hightailed it out of here when the dragon showed up. The Blades should have a few minutes of safety to regroup.

"What the hell happened?" Perric said from where he sat with his back against a giant tree. Jileli sat next to him, with Ayre and Lithia nearby.

"It would appear we were attacked by a dragon," Ayre said in his normal sarcastic tone. "I thought you had noticed the giant drake trying to eat you."

Perric sighed.

Jileli patted him on the arm. "Thank you for carrying me. I don't think I would have made it."

Perric grinned like a schoolboy. "You are more than welcome. We are a team and protect each other."

"We are, but what I want to know is why the dragon is trying to kill us, or is it after the wizard?" Saria asked the group. She knew no one had that particular answer, but she felt better asking it out loud. "This makes three times it has been in the same place as us, and this isn't exactly a small country. One time near Moonbourne and then in two different towns."

"Could the bounty be a trap like the bounty for Chaos Clan?" Jileli asked. "Could the Skull Posse be using it to kill us?"

"There aren't enough of Skull Posse left to fill a cup, let alone control a dragon," Ayre said. His dagger flickered through his fingers at an ever-increasing pace.

"What if whoever gave Skull Posse the death marker can control a dragon?" Lithia said.

"I can't imagine anyone alive today able to control a dragon." Saria briefly thought of Brar Opalback, but the sorceress hadn't been angry at the Blades when Skull Posse had attacked them. She wouldn't have them marked for assassination given she needed the Blades to fetch the orb. Saria highly doubted Brar would have kept something like a killer pet dragon a secret for this long, only to bust it out because Saria ticked her off.

Lithia shook her head. "This bounty is cursed."

"Agreed," Perric said morosely. "I didn't even get to finish my last ale."

"I don't think it's that complicated," Ayre finally said. "It's like Jileli suggested earlier. My guess is the wizard's spell is attracting the dragon. The magic is so powerful the drake is attracted to it. The only thing that can challenge a dragon is potent magic, so dragons view those magic users as threats. Elladon Kane's spell on those innkeepers must be very strong, the type of magic the dragons associate with those who used to hunt them. Either way, we need to rid ourselves of the bounty."

"That doesn't explain the first sighting," Saria reminded him. Could it be that simple? The dragon thought Elladon Kane's spells were a threat? But how had Kane managed to live as long as he had, if his magic was strong enough to attract dragons that were previously thought to have died out?

"We did have the bounty parchment with us then," Jileli mused. "But it wasn't triggered until we showed it to the barkeeps. That is robust magic, to last so long."

"I think we should burn the bounty," Lithia said. "Good riddance to it."

"No, we need to keep the bounty." Jileli paused for a long moment. "I might be able to use it to unravel the spell so we can see the true intentions behind it."

"Or it could bring the dragon back," Perric said.

"Another protejel might protect us," Lithia said. "It did the first time. There is one within a day's journey but it's in the opposite direction of Yllle Serinis."

"Then we shouldn't go there. I want to finish this bounty. Once we get our hands on Kane, I plan on getting the truth about this whole ordeal even if I have to beat it out of him," Ayre said.

"Will the elves even let us into their realm?" Lithia's gaze flickered to Jileli. "Two of us are considered heretics and might be killed on sight."

"You have nothing to worry about," Ayre said. "We will demand sanctuary, which will stay their hands until we've met with the royal attorney. Given the circumstances, we should be fine."

"Should?" Saria asked.

"What happens if we aren't?" Lithia asked, her voice thick with worry.

Ayre shrugged. "Then we will all travel to the next life together."

27

After the second day of hiking, they camped in the forest for the rest of the night. Saria took the last guard shift, so she had time to review the day ahead. From her calculations, Yllle Serinis was two to three days away. Traveling through the forest was slow going, but if you wanted to visit the elves, you spent a lot of time in the forest. Their cities were enchanted so that they were difficult to find. Ayre had pointed out on Selwyn's map where each of the cities were, so she had a rough idea.

When the sun came up, they started off in the general direction of the city. Ayre led the way since he had been there many times.

"What is Yllle Serinis like?" Saria asked him while they journeyed. The thief's mood had gone sour, and each mile seemed to put him in a worse one. "You lived there?"

He sighed. "I did when I was a child. Yllle Serinis translates to sun among the trees. It is a beautiful city of silver archways and terrace gardens. The Queen rules from the palace there. The politics are treacherous and deviously played out. I had a run-in with the captain of the royal guards, who took exception to me sleeping with his wife."

"I could see why."

"And his daughter." Ayre glanced at Saria and then added, "Not at the same time. That would be very wrong."

"It would be disturbing, at least."

"He sent assassins after me, but when their heads kept being delivered to him, he lost interest, or at least the assassins decided other jobs were far easier."

"Who was the noble?"

"His name was Galen Magrel. He was the royal guard captain for her royal majesty. Good with a blade, but not overly bright."

"Assassination seems a bit harsh for an affair." How had the elves lived for so long with all of the underhanded politics and killings? It seemed they would have reduced their own populations without help from the monsters.

"He's a pompous ass. The Queen exiled me to assuage his bruised ego. Never liked the man, but his wife was lovely and very enthusiastic. His daughter was as well, but far less skilled. I should have made a public apology, taken my lumps, and gone on with things, but I was very young and truly hated the man. I've been fighting monsters and bedding whoever would have me ever since."

Saria laughed. Ayre was accurate. He'd been a complete reprobate when they first met. He took a liking to Saria, and, after a while, they formed the Blades, recruited a few others, and started tackling bounties. Five years later, and they were still going, and Ayre was only about half reprobate. They'd lost a few members along the way to retirement and unfortunate events, but Ayre and Saria were still a team. Perric had been with them for three years or so. Now they had two new members and a dragon trying to kill them. Sanctuary in the land of the elves sounded pretty good.

"Were you always so levelheaded and sensible?" Ayre asked. "You'd never have been drummed out of town for sleeping with the wrong person. You learned to fight and joined the Duke's guards when you were, what, eighteen?"

"I was a street rat and tried to steal from Regina. Instead of cutting off my hand, she gave me a choice. Prison or join the guards. I took the easy way out."

"And before that?" He cast a quick glance at her as they treaded side by side between enormous trees. "You've really never talked about that time in your life."

Saria wasn't sure if he was interested or changing the subject. It was true they knew a lot about each other, but neither of them had been hugely forthcoming about their earliest years. "That's because I don't remember much. I was an orphan. I vaguely remember running with gangs of kids in the streets, but that was twenty years ago. Regina caught me trying to snatch her purse, beat me, then gave me the option to train to be a guard, or she'd put me on hard labor.."

"Not much of a choice."

"No." Her memories of the time before she was about sixteen years old were fuzzy and confusing, some with a distinct tinge of pain and fear. "I'd already escaped one orphanage. I wasn't going back. They tormented the kids or sold them off to rich households for sport."

"Nasty business there," Ayre said. His eyes held hers for a moment, and she could tell he was upset for her. "Here I had a life of plenty while you struggled to stay alive. I was a spoiled brat, so my current situation is a culmination of my bad choices and selfish behavior."

Ayre's words hit her like a comet. What was awaiting Ayre that he had become so introspective and eager to analyze their childhoods together? "We all do what we think is best at the time. Fortunately, we found each other and the Blades. We have our own family now."

Ayre nodded but didn't say anything. They walked in silence for the next hour. His eyes were everywhere and his dagger was out. "We are getting close now. Do not say anything if we are greeted by any elves. Let me speak. My people are touchy at the best of times, and any perceived slight can be deadly."

"So, it's not just you," Perric said with a grin.

"I'm the fun, lovable one among the elves," Ayre said with a mock bow. Perric laughed.

They continued on for a while when Ayre raised his hand to stop the group. The breeze carried the fresh scent of the forest and the chirps of the birds flying around overhead. They all stayed quiet, waiting for an explanation.

Guards in ceremonial armor stepped out of thin air to surround the Blades. The lead guard said, "Lay down your weapons, you are trespassing on elvish soil. You will be allowed to turn back, or we will take you as prisoners to be tried in front of the court."

"I demand sanctuary. We are travelers in need of the protection of the elven empire."

"Isn't this grand?" another voice said as a newcomer appeared. "The wayward son has returned."

"Greetings, Galen Magrel. I hope your wife and daughter are well."

Oh, fuck.

28

Galen Magrel stepped forward and slapped Ayre across the face. "You'd do well to still your tongue, boy. In case you haven't heard, you've been exiled."

Saria tensed, ready to fight. If Ayre pulled steel, it would get messy, but they were a troop and would stick together.

"I'm sure your family wept at the thought of being left alone with you." Ayre rubbed his cheek.

"Always quick with the witless responses. You are trespassing on elven soil. I'm arresting you on the Queen's warrant. Take the kaetter to the cells. We do not abide their type. The others may depart," Galen said, turning to leave. His guards closed in to follow orders.

"We were instructed to come here by the wizard Elladon Kane. We are under his protection," Ayre said. "You might want to think twice before accosting me and mine."

Galen turned around slowly. He studied Ayre for a long time. No doubt he was trying to figure out if Ayre told the truth.

Saria had met plenty of pompous, spoiled men in her life.

This one was no exception. Instead of addressing the issues of his wife's infidelity and fixing it, he blamed someone else. If he'd been a good husband, nothing Ayre did could have caused his wife to stray.

As for the daughter, well, Saria granted she didn't know the whole story there. Were elves monogamous or did they have many rules around dalliances? No elves she'd ever met had given her the impression they were any different than humans in that regard.

"You could arrest us, imprison or run off my troop, but what do you think such a powerful man as the wizard might do to you when you've interfered with his plan?"

Galen pursed his lips. "You have always been a liar and betrayer. Why should I trust your word now?"

"You are correct," Ayre said with a shrug. "I am a liar, thief, and fornicator, as you well know, but why would I return to Yllle Serinis with the knowledge you'll try to convince the Queen to execute me?"

"You bring up a good point," Galen said, tapping his chin with his finger. "Here's another. If you're lying, allowing you into Yllle Serinis could be seen as a betrayal of my solemn duty. I have no desire to join you on the execution platform."

"Sir, what should we do?" one of the guards asked. Some of them had their blades out, while some left theirs sheathed.

"You'll wait for orders," Galen snapped at him.

The man stiffened and saluted the guard captain. "As you wish."

"This is exactly the type of behavior that drove your wife into my arms, Galen. Tsk, tsk. Well, your daughter just hates you, so it is easy to see why—"

A slap rang out as Galen struck Ayre much harder. "Watch your tongue or I'll cut it out." The man's words were a hiss of fury and rage.

Saria stayed silent, but Ayre's only plan seemed to be to

get them all killed. She kept her hand on her sword but hoped it didn't come to that. He had warned them all to let him speak, to hold their tongues, and she had to trust that he knew what he was about.

Ayre wiped the blood from the edge of his mouth. "Good to see your temper is well controlled. Galen Magrel, I name you a coward who is not fit to wear the royal livery. I demand to be taken to the Queen to redress my status as exiled."

Galen broke into a hearty laugh. "Oof, that is rich. No, I think my men will slay you all, and I will present her royal majesty with your head."

Saria gripped the hilt of her sword. Perric's hands twitched, but he stayed still. Lithia and Jileli looked mortified.

The twelve guards glanced back and forth between them. None of them had made any moves towards the Shadow Blades, yet.

Ayre's daggers were in his hands. "You know the codes. As I see it you have two choices, and one ends up with you having to explain why your guards are dead."

Magrel's eyes darted around the clearing. A deepening frown crossed his features as his eyes took in the Blades.

"You might best us, but…" Ayre drew out the sentence with a smile.

"I challenge you to a duel," Galen Magrel said in a haughty tone. "If you best me, then you and your friends will be granted sanctuary in the Eternal Groves."

Ayre straightened his jerkin and saluted Magrel. "I guess I'll accept your generous offer. I will send you to the pit with the rest of the unworthy."

"Prepare the trial amphitheater. I will teach this whelp not to question his betters."

Well, Ayre had gotten them into Yllle Serinis in their

search for this damnedable bounty. Would they make it back out alive?

"orm up around the prisoners," the guard captain said.

The soldiers ringed the Blades, eyes straight ahead. Their precision impressed Saria, though she'd rather be watching from the outside, not a prisoner.

"You," Galen said, pointing at one of the guards. "Run ahead and have the arena prepared. We will be along shortly."

The guard saluted and ran through the veil and vanished from view.

If the elves had this strong of magic, why weren't they fighting the monsters instead of hiding in the forest? The rest of the world was bleeding and dying while they were safe here. Just like the dwarves locked themselves behind impenetrable walls, and the shadow fae retreated below ground. The humans and other weaker races were the ones bearing the brunt of the monster infestation, like the disposable front line of infantry.

The irony that the races who were best equipped to handle the monsters were the ones who ran away and hid was not lost on Saria, but the display of their magics and skilled armed forces brought it home to her in a new way.

Saria felt her anger rising, at both the elves and Ayre, but tamped it down. Ayre must have a plan, or at least she hoped he did, and she needed to follow his lead.

The strange procession set off. Saria felt a slight tingle on her skin as they passed through the veil. Jileli gasped like she'd been struck, but a quick glance assured her the mage was through and walking in front of Perric.

After a few minutes in the woods, they came upon a road. Galen directed them onto it, and they walked for another two hours in absolute silence. If Ayre had any more digs for Galen, he kept them to himself.

The city emerged from the forest, and Saria sighed. She had lived all her life in the real world, but the elves lived somewhere else entirely. Spires of white stone rose into the air while arching bridges etched with gold spanned between them. Terraces full of flowers decorated every building, and the grounds were covered with plants and ornamental trees.

Paradise.

Galen took a hard right before they reached the city proper and led them around the outskirts. Saria lost track of the time, enamored with the beauty of Yllle Serinis. They finally arrived at a huge amphitheater that descended to a large platform in the middle. Stone benches with seating for thousands ringed the stage. People milled in from the far side of the structure. The people were as beautifully dressed as the city itself. Citizens decked out in every color under the rainbow drifted down the stairs to take a seat to watch the spectacle unfold.

"Put them there," Galen said to the lead guard, pointing at the top row of seats. "If any try to interfere, kill them, especially her."

He pointed directly at Jileli.

Ayre turned to the Blades. "I'll give him a couple of scars to brag about later and then we'll find the wizard. Galen is all bluster and drama."

Saria opened her mouth, but a small shake of the head from Ayre silenced her.

"Mind he doesn't poison his blade," Lithia whispered anyway, eyeing the crowd with wariness. "Honor duels as we know are not always honorable."

The thief walked down the stairs. He called over his shoulder. "Galen, are you coming? I'd like to pay your wife a visit once I'm done with this."

The guard captain's face turned beet red, but he stomped down the stairs, unbuckling his jacket as he went.

They reached the platform, and the captain had stripped down to his shirt. His sword was in his hand. An older man strode to the center and bowed to each of the duelists. If he spoke to them, Saria couldn't hear it. He straightened and raised his voice.

"Today, we will bear witness to this duel. Guard Captain Magrel has accused Ayre of…" He looked to Ayre for him to fill in the rest of his name.

"Just Ayre."

The man gave him a curt nod. "Ayre of fornication and cuckoldry. The fight is to first blood."

"No," Galen said loudly so all could hear. "He has wronged me and my family, and he is an embarrassment to the entire nation. We will fight to the death."

"Do you agree, Ayre? You may refuse, but then your party will suffer the consequences you agreed to."

"Death it is. I'll be sure to comfort your widow and your daughter," Ayre said, then paused. "Quite possibly at the same time. That would be fun."

Saria was surprised that the guard captain's face could get any redder, but it did. "Move," he snarled.

"It is agreed. Let the duel commence." The man stepped quickly out of the way, but Galen almost impaled him in his rush to get to Ayre.

Ayre stood still until the last possible second, then shifted and kicked Galen in the side of the knee. He stumbled, but caught his balance. He slashed his sword at Ayre's head, but the thief had already moved. He kicked Galen in the ass, sending him sprawling. The crowd laughed.

Ayre took center stage and waited for the sputtering man to rise. He straightened and proceeded with more caution. He advanced on Ayre, who could have been standing in line for the jakes.

One day his ego was going to get him killed. He was being sloppy and showboating, and if this went poorly, the Blades had no way out. Galen wasn't a slouch with the blade. Ayre needed to be careful. He was gambling with all their lives.

Galen's sword flickered, and the tip slashed toward Ayre's knees.

Ayre hopped back, and the sword whistled through thin air.

Galen growled, thrusting the sword, but he twisted it at the last second and nicked Ayre's left arm above the wrist.

"Too bad it's not to first blood," Ayre said with a smirk.

The guard captain smiled. "Your pride will be the death of you, boy."

"I've heard that before, or was it my mouth? I can't quite keep track."

Perric muttered, "Both," under his breath. Saria fought not to laugh. She heard a few of the guards snicker behind them. Ayre really needed to get his head in the fight because arrogance did not win battles.

Galen advanced, his sword blurring with the speed and ferocity of his attacks. Ayre blocked, parried, and side-stepped them with ease. She had seen Ayre fight before, many times, but this demonstration revealed that she'd never seen him fight at all. He was so accomplished it was as if Galen was a novice, yet anyone could see that Galen was skilled enough that he would best nearly all who came before him.

Galen's mistake was so minor, only a sword master would have noticed. He overextended his reach by a fraction of an inch. Ayre dropped his off-hand blade, latched onto his opponent's arm, and threw the guard captain over his hip.

Galen squawked as he took flight. He landed hard on his back. Before he could move, Ayre pounced, pinning the man to the floor with his knee. Ayre's dagger pressed against the guard captain's throat. "Yield, or I'll send you to the pit."

"Enough!" a voice shouted. Ayre's head came up. A stunning woman with a crown and a scepter stood at the top of the stairs, flanked by a royal guard.

"All hail, Queen Thaciona, royal ruler of the Yllle Serinis. Sovereign of the Eternal Groves," the crowd said in unison. All of her subjects bowed before her.

"Of all my sons, it is always you, Ayre, who finds their way into trouble," she said in a motherly voice.

The Queen was Ayre's mother?

30

W hy, hello, Mother," Ayre said in a flippant tone. "You look well."

The older man who was refereeing the duel snarled, "Show proper respect to the Queen."

Thaciona shook her head. Her long silver hair reached her waist. She wore a lavender gown trimmed with silver embroidery and carried a staff with a gem larger than Saria's fist. Every ounce of Saria wanted to bow to her royal majesty, but she wasn't an elf, nor was she was a prisoner.

"Why have you returned and why, pray tell, are you trying to kill my guard captain?"

"Mother, I am on a quest, and it brought me to your door. Galen and I were talking over old times. He was just telling me about his lovely wife and daughter."

A twitter of soft giggles went through the crowd. No wonder the guard captain hated Ayre so much. He'd made him the laughingstock of the city.

For the second time.

"Not this again," Thaciona said with a frown. "Captain,

you are forbidden from touching my son or his friends, do you understand?"

"Yes, my Queen," he said. Clearly the Queen could change the rules of duels as it suited her.

"Ayre, let him go, please." Ayre did as he was asked. Galen got to his feet and retrieved his fallen sword.

"You are dismissed, Captain." Thaciona turned and spoke to her guard, who returned the way they came. She descended the stairs as if she floated above them. When she reached the platform, she addressed the crowd. "The duel is over. Please return to your day. May the light bless you all."

When the crowd had dispersed, she called to the guards. "Please send Ayre's team down to join us, and then you're dismissed."

"But your Majesty," one very brave guard said. "There are two kaetter with him. We should stay to protect you."

She laughed softly. "Ladies, do I have any worries about you harming me?"

Jileli and Lithia both shook their heads. They didn't speak, but if that was nerves or Ayre's request not to speak, Saria didn't know.

"There you go," Thaciona said simply. "We are all on the same side. You are dismissed. If the rest of you would kindly join my son and I to discuss what brings you to our fair city?"

Saria stood and led the Blades down the stairs. They reached the platform, and all bowed to Queen Thaciona.

"There is no need for that," she said with an offhanded wave. "Ayre, why have you come back? You left me no choice but to exile you. The captain is correct that your life should be forfeited."

"I'm sorry, Mother, that I've embarrassed you. It wasn't my intention. I did not want to spill Galen's blood to satisfy his ego, but he demanded a duel to the death."

"I gathered that much," the queen said, looking like the

most beautiful, and long-suffering, mother in all the world. "And how did you fare these years?"

"I plied my skills to defending the helpless citizenry from the monsters outside the Eternal Groves, of course." Saria did not correct Ayre, since he had only begun to fight monsters after joining forces with her. "I met up with Saria, the leader of the Shadow Blades, and have fought by her side against the monsters."

"You have my thanks, Lady Saria."

"Just Saria, your Majesty," Saria said, bowing her head slightly. "I am a warrior doing what I can to protect the innocents of this world." She didn't add, unlike you, any more than she corrected Ayre's version of events. Her friend had been raised by people who thought nothing of the chaos outside their walls or the good they could be doing. It had taken him some time to come around.

Ayre gestured to Perric. "This is Perric, holy knight of Drohara. Next to him is our mage Jileli and our cousin Lithia, the archer."

"It is a pleasure to meet you all," Thaciona said with a soft smile. "My thanks for keeping my son safe."

"We all keep each other safe," Saria said.

Ayre gestured toward the city proper. "We have come to find the wizard Elladon Kane. Is he in Yllle Serinis?"

"He is. Tell me of your quest."

Ayre glanced at Saria. She took the hint and reviewed the trip from Moonbourne to Coldbrook, the fight with the gnolls, the dragon attack, and their flight to Yllle Serinis. She left out parts about the search for Talos and some of the more questionable things that had happened.

"You've been busy," Thaciona said after Saria had finished. "May I see this parchment?"

Saria pulled the bounty from her pouch and handed it to

her royal majesty. "We have some concerns that the magic in it may be attracting the red dragon."

"That is not a concern in my city," the queen said, showing little surprise they had tangled with a dragon. She took it and examined it for a long time. Her eyes seemed to glaze over as she studied it. She handed it back to Saria. "That was very intricate spell work, Elladon."

"Why thank you, your Majesty. I thought it was a nice bit of craft," an unknown voice said from the top of the stairs.

Saria looked up to see a man wearing a dark blue robe with white at the collar and cuffs. He had shaggy brown hair and walked with a wooden staff. He proceeded to stomp down the stairs, an ogre compared to the soft grace of the Queen.

"Wizard Elladon Kane?" Saria asked. Questions flooded her mind, but she blurted out the biggest one. "Why did you bring us all the way here? What do you expect from us?"

"What do I expect?" Elladon said, placing his open hand over his heart. "Why, I expect you to set things right and kill Brar Opalback."

ACKNOWLEDGMENTS

This marks my 10th published book. Wow!

One of the few bright spots of 2023 has been getting to work on the Shadow Blades novellas. Being able to dive into the world of Providence and take Saria and the Blades on epic adventures has been a great diversion from our own troubled world. There is so much bad news in the world right now. I wanted to provide my readers with a fun adventure with great characters and a fast-paced story that keeps you turning pages.

Did I succeed?

If I did, please leave a review. Hell, if I didn't, leave a review. Goodreads and Amazon reviews truly help sell books which lets me write more books.

Jody Wallace did the edits on the book. This novella was challenging with as complex as the plot gets. She worked though the entire series ensuring all three installments were cohesive and could be followed across multiple titles. Not an easy feat.

Natania Barron designed the cover which is simple and elegant. She's also an amazing author. Nobody should be that talented, but she is wonderful to work with and I love her artwork.

Emily Leverett did the copy/proofreading on the book. She also caught a couple things the other 5 passes missed. It is impossible to find all typos, but it's like the Hunger Games. If they can survive the purge, they get to live.

John Hartness did the formatting, which takes a word doc

and produces amazing looking books. He takes extra time to do the little things, like the sword icons and the extra design openings.

A special thank you to Regina Kirby (the Mistress of Bounties) who won a charity auction so her name would be used in the book and now she is immortalized in the Shadow Blades world forever. You never know once you get going what's going to happen with my writing. What started off as a bit role turned into a pretty major character.

Writing is a solidary pursuit and comes with a lot of rejection and long hours. Fortunately, I've found myself in the middle of an amazing community of writers and fans who make things fun and are there on the days when things aren't so fun. I'm going to mention as many as I can, but if your name isn't here, it is because my brain is still dealing with COVID's Swiss cheese aftereffects. To start I'd like to thank Joe and Mary Mayo for sticking with me through all these years and a lot of ups and downs. Joelle Reizes, Jim Nettles, Darin Kennedy, Leslie Gould, and Melissa McArthur meet up most weeks to talk writing and other topics. It always brightens my day. April Baker, Kiersten and Seth Keipper, Wanda Harward, and Gerrit Overeen have been doing Books & Beer on Monday nights with me. Lots of fun to hangout, drink beer, and sell a couple of books. Adrianne McDonald has been instrumental in helping me get through the last year both from her friendship and her immense knowledge and understanding. Nicole and Wes Smith, Tally and Rachel Johnson, Jessica Nettles, Allie Charlesworth, Cisca Smalls, Sarah Sover, Sue Phillips, Jesse Adams, Nancy Knight, James and Jennifer Liang, Mera Rose, and many, many others have become part of my convention family. Last, but certainly, not least, a huge thank you to Dino Hicks and the amazing friend he is, not only to me, but all the indie authors who he befriends.

My family is the reason I can do what I do. They are amazing. Emily and Nicholas are always reminding me that I'm Dad first, writer second. I'd have it no other way. Blaze reminds me to give him treats and take him out. He says that is his way of getting me to take breaks. My wife Hope is the glue that keeps everything together. I have no idea how she works a full-time job, coaches, and publishes non-fiction books and still has time to be the most amazing wife and mother anyone could ask for.

Of course, I would like to thank you, the reader. I hope my writing makes your day a little better, allows you to forget about the bad things and escape into diverse worlds with unique characters. Without you, my stories would just be words on a page.

Until next book,

Patrick

November 2023

ABOUT THE AUTHOR

Patrick is the author of the award-winning Darkest Storm Series published by Falstaff Books. Other titles include Never Steal From Dragons and Watchers of Astaria series from Distracted Dragon Press. Other publications include Fairy Films: Wee Folk on the Big Screen, a collection of fairy essays. Patrick is a member of SFWA.

An avid gadget user, Patrick is also the Director of Technology Services for Author's Essentials LLC providing solutions and advice for writing professionals. Patrick writings delve into software, hardware, social media, and all things web-related. The primary focus of Author's Essentials is how and when to employ technology to enhance your writing process.

Patrick resides in Charlotte, NC with his wife and two children. In his spare time, he's a PC gamer, homebrewer, 3D printer enthusiast, and DIYer. You can usually find him in the Hearthstone Tavern or wandering Azeroth as a Blood Elf Warlock in the evenings.

You can find out more at https://linktr.ee/patrickdugan

ALSO BY PATRICK DUGAN

The Shadow Blade Series

The Ashen Orb Bounty

The Dragon's Wrath Bounty

The Wayward Mage Bounty

Pixiepunk Series

Never Steal from Dragons

Watchers of Astaria Series

Fate & Flux – Prequel

Of Cogs & Conjuring

Pistols & Potions

Machines & Monsters

The Darkest Storm Series

Storm Forged

Unbreakable Storm

Storm Shattered

Made in the USA
Columbia, SC
20 February 2024

32037360R00105